"The stories he presents are not spectacular, are not extravaganzas or pretentious and inordinate piety. They are stories of real people in the world of reality. People who quarreled, forgave and were forgiven. People who smoked, danced, cursed, drank liquor, went to war, segregated and sometimes messed around on Saturday night. Knowing somehow that they were sinners in it all, and that grace knows no bounds. Grace. Unconditional. Amazing."
—**Will D. Campbell, in *Southern Quarterly***

"Here are presented the foibles, subterfuges, necessary illusions, and faith by which the 'down home' characters survive their pasts to inform and enrich their present lives. . . . This, finally, is the charm and the strength of [*Survivors and Others*]: that they are 'always on the side of life.'"
—**Louise N. Soldani, in *Christianity and Literature***

"His stories are told in a cozy conversational tone that resembles but transcends the pettiness of gossip. We are given a perspective rather than just a peek into the lives of residents of Woodville. . . . Every story is built up out of shared experience."
—**Bill King, in *The Jackson Sun***

"Drake's stories bear witness to a childhood ear finely tuned to the stories and conversations of the older people around him. His stories are honest and natural—hallmarks of a fine Southern writer."
—**Lana S. Dixon, in *Tennessee Librarian***

"His stories represent an effort to gain health and wholeness, to complete the life narrative—the basis and goal of good fiction, psychoanalysis and religion. Drake's stories encourage us to engage in a similarly difficult but potentially rewarding meditation."
—**Lewis A. Lawson, *The Christian Century***

"Readers who have followed Robert Drake's work for the last thirty years have come to each new book of stories with a set of expectations: that it will be rich in characterization (communicated primarily through *talk*), that it will favor anecdote and observation over plot, and that it will be cast as first-person reminiscence. The most recent collection, *My Sweetheart's House*, will not disappoint."
—**James H. Justus, *Modern Age***

What Will You Do for an Encore?
and Other Stories

Also by Robert Drake

FICTION

Amazing Grace (1965; 25th anniversary edition 1990)

The Single Heart (1971)

The Burning Bush (1975)

Survivors and Others (1987)

My Sweetheart's House: Memories, Fictions (1993)

CRITICISM

Flannery O'Connor
Contemporary Writers in Christian Perspective (1966)

MEMOIR

The Home Place: A Memory and a Celebration (1980)

What Will You Do for an Encore?
and Other Stories

ROBERT DRAKE

Mercer University Press

Macon, Georgia 1996

ISBN 0-86554-523-5

What Will You Do for an Encore?
and Other Stories
by Robert Drake

Copyright 1996
Mercer University Press, Macon, Georgia 31210 USA
All rights reserved.
Printed in the United States of America.

———

Some of these stories appeared originally in
The Chattahoochee Review, The Christian Century,
CrossRoads, Image, Modern Age, Soundings, and *Southern Partisan.*

"The Methodist Church, the Democratic Party, and the St. Louis Cardinals" is
copyrighted 1994 by the Christian Century Foundation, and is reprinted by
permission from the August 24-31, 1994 issue of *The Christian Century.*

———

The paper used in this publication meets the minimum requirements
of American National Standard for Information Services—
Permanence of Paper for Printed Library Materials,
ANSI Z39.48-1984

Library of Congress Cataloging-in-Publication Data

Drake, Robert, 1930–
    What will you do for an encore? and other stories / by Robert Drake.
        x + 149   6x9"
    ISBN 0-86554-523-5 (alk. paper)
    1. Southern States—Social life and customs—Fiction. 2. City and town life
        —Southern States—Fiction.   I. Title.
    PS3554.R237W48   1996
    813'.54—dc20   96-30808
                                                                              CIP

———

Front cover photograph, "Epps Field, 1937," © 1996 by Roy Ward.
Reproduced by arrangement with Roy Ward.
Author photograph, "Robert Drake," © 1996 Michael O'Brien.
Used with permission of the photographer.

Contents

I want to thank the John C. Hodges Better English Fund
at the University of Tennessee for assisting
with the publication of this collection,

and

I also want to express my thanks
to Kay Gardner, Lisa Lance, and Sheri Stephens
for their expert typing.

Our world seems to go from one crisis to another, maybe one anticlimax to another, with all its leaders and pundits shouting "Lo here" and "Lo there," always proclaiming the apocalypse in every new home remedy that comes along. But finally they all run out of gas because it just doesn't seem to work that way but rather in the returning and rest wherein we are saved, in the quietness and confidence wherein lies our strength. And we begin to have some idea that what we really have been seeking is not a *climax*, which, like a drug, necessitates literally an infinite series of encores, but a *celebration*, ultimate and eternal. And who needs an encore then?

—R. D.

Knoxville

September, 1995

For

Laura Garnet, Margaret, and Frances

What Will You Do for an Encore?

For some years now I've been saying that if I ever wrote my autobiography, I should want to call it *What Will You Do for an Encore*? Because that has always seemed to me the fundamental question about most matters in life that are often the greatest frustrations for most of us. I remember when I got a new puppy in the first grade—nothing "well bred" about him, just a common ordinary garden variety of "rat dog." And I thought he was as cute as a button. But what could you do with him finally? You couldn't *talk* to him, and you certainly couldn't *read* to him. And you couldn't play with him *all* the time. And when you did, you always had to run in the house afterwards, I thought, and wash your hands: I was beginning to find out about *germs* and was naturally somewhat fearful of the whole business (enemies you couldn't *see*) and therefore quick to exploit my new-found knowledge. My father of course thought the whole business was absurd: any real *boy* ought to have a dog, of course, but he also ought to know that the fleas, to say nothing of the germs, were part of the deal and simply take the whole business in his stride. Why, he said, he even *slept* with his dog when he was growing up, though of course he never let his mother know about it.

It was the same way about other things you wanted: so you finally got a new book you had been longing for, well what could you *do* with it once you had read it and found out how it all "came out"—just read it over and over again? I even thought the *possession* of books a mixed blessing (where would you put them all when you had read them?); it was what was *in* the books that I cared for so why not just check them out of the library and return them when you were done reading them? But then I thought it must be that way about objects of beauty and luxury too: what could you do with them after you finally got them—just sit there and admire them for the rest of your life? That sounded like a pretty dull business to me, whether it was a beautiful painting or a new house, even a new car. Whatever you wanted and wanted badly in this world, it looked like sooner or later, it wore out and there you were left with it on your hands and probably bored as all get out. Was it the law of diminishing returns? The very act of achievement, the moment of triumph itself had a built-in anticlimax, and afterwards it was downhill all the way. Later, after I had learned a little physics, I thought it all had something to do with the second law of thermodynamics, but I couldn't get much further than that. It all remained a great mystery.

Even Heaven itself sounded like it might be that way. O.K., so you made it up there and didn't get turned away from the gate by St. Peter; and when the roll was called up yonder, you'd be there, actually *saved*, as the Baptists always put it. Well, so what? Did you just lie around playing the harp all the time from then on or walking up and down the golden stairs? As I recall, Mark Twain himself raised questions about such matters. What, he wanted know, would you *do* up there? Or again, maybe it was like what Thoreau said about the popular clamor to build a telegraph wire from Maine to Texas: maybe, he said, Maine and Texas had nothing to say to each other. Even God, if and when you ever had the chance to speak to Him, might have finally run out of things to say. And there you would be with all eternity on your hands and nothing to do. You might even wonder whether or not the *eternal rest* preachers were always talking about as one of the gratifications of the afterlife would be such a great idea. As for me, I thought I would go crazy with nothing to do but just sit there and hold my hands. And certainly, nobody was ever going to pay me to sit there and look pretty.

But of course all this didn't mean I was ready to go to the Bad Place, as I called it in my childhood: eternal punishment didn't sound at all like an attractive alternative. And the idea of having to go before the Judgment Seat to find out whether I was *worthy* of Heaven didn't sound like such a fine prospect either: I never was any good at winning races or any other kind of contest. Really, I even sometimes thought of myself as a born loser, and I was fat and wore braces on my teeth and took piano lessons and didn't feel like I would ever be "chosen" for anything. It might not be as bad as leprosy, but it was quite effectual in bringing about an isolation which was far from splendid.

Frankly, it all sounded something like a sad prospect whichever way you looked at it: you were damned if you did and damned if you didn't. But one idea did seem less ominous, maybe even something like fun, though you didn't hear much about it from the Baptists and such like, who were always great on *excluding* rather than *including*. (For that matter, they could usually give you the day and the hour when they were saved, like they had some sort of contract with the Authorities "up there." But then I always thought we all couldn't be like St. Paul on the road to Damascus; the lives of most of us weren't nearly so dramatic.)

Maybe it was all going to be something like a big party, where you were supposed to *enjoy* yourself. The New Testament especially was full of parties, feasts, banquets, even weddings; and the part I liked best was that *everybody* was invited—well, saved if you wanted to put it that way. And the only thing that could keep you out was if you just didn't choose to accept the invitation. And that maybe was always within your power: God, the ultimate host, didn't want you around if you were there only under duress. (That was maybe what free will was all about.) And really, He was so anxious to have a big crowd, He would send His servants— whoever they were, saints? apostles?—out into the highways and byways and *compel* all the pouters and other such disaffected folks to come in. Well, I thought that was certainly a fine alternative to the eternal singing of hymns (and usually the bloodier the better) and shouting and carrying on around the Throne of Grace. And of course there would be lots of things to eat *and* drink—and no Welch's grape juice either. (The story about Christ's first miracle was one of my favorites, especially when it said He "adorned and beautified" the occasion with his presence. And I always wondered whether Billy Graham had ever adorned and beautified anything with *his* presence, much less shouted for joy about the Good News or anything else: his favorite word always seemed to be "warn.")

When I was a child, it usually scared me to read the Bible: most of the Old Testament, with all its "shall nots," always made me feel like I wouldn't make the grade. (And it certainly looked like there were fewer souls "saved" than there were "chosen.") But every now and then it did seem that this "party" version of Heaven was often on the side of pleasure: people even got their feet washed and their heads anointed with oil on occasion. And when I got older, I read about Dr. Johnson saying that a man who wouldn't mind his belly would hardly mind anything else, so I decided there wasn't anything inherently wrong with the things of this world. And I began to feel a lot better about the whole pleasure principle: it had always seemed to me that most of the world around me thought that if something made you feel good, it was probably bad for you physically or morally or in some other way.

But still there were doubts: if that was the way Heaven really operated, what would you do after you finished your supper and all the rest of it? Wouldn't you just want to curl up and go to sleep? And what about all the conversation with God or the other guests? (I especially wanted to have a long talk with Bach and Jane Austen.) For the most part, it didn't particularly sound like any feast of reason and flow of souls. Wouldn't you finally tire of that also? Was there anything that finally didn't "run down," anything that finally didn't become a bore? (Never any encores and always the second law of thermodynamics again.)

Even seeing *Gone with the Wind* and *The Wizard of Oz* every day would get tiresome; maybe, as my mother said, there were times when you could even get too much ice cream (though I did find that hard to believe). What was there left for you to *do* then if you got everything you wanted, even everything you prayed for? And of course that might be a joker too: I once heard a red-hot evangelist proclaim that you'd better be mighty careful what you prayed for because you were liable to get it! I suppose I've been worried about that sort of thing all my life, and I've never really been able to come to terms with the matter; that's why I still don't know what you can do for an encore so much of the time, how you can top your latest success. Like in the old days in Hollywood: they used to say you were only as good as your last picture. Would you be bored even in Heaven?

Well, I still don't have the answer to all this; but as I've grown older, I've begun to have what my mother used to call a sneaking idea that to ask this question ("What will you *do*?") is, in some measure, to answer it. Because maybe in Heaven unlike elsewhere we aren't supposed to *do* anything, in the sense of working or performing for God because that's not what we were created for: after all, God is not an employer. (Indeed, my old friend, Cleanth Brooks, distinguished scholar and critic, once told me that he thought the real trouble in *Paradise Lost* starts when Eve suggests to Adam that they go trim up more bushes and vines than necessary.) God doesn't *need* that, and man is presumptuous to think so. And maybe all He wants is for man to accept the gift, the invitation which He has so freely given; we don't have to, indeed cannot *do* anything *for* God. Perhaps that's the trouble with justification by works and the very thing that makes His news so Good—and indeed, the only kind that's valid and true. Perhaps as Thoreau observed about much of the so-called "news" our world yearns, even lusts for, it's finally nothing but gossip.

I think somehow all this is connected with something Mrs. Hardy, my high school senior English teacher, said in class one day. She was a good strong Methodist and, I think, very much an includer rather than an excluder. (She couldn't have taught school all those years without being one: any teacher knows that.) And she never sounded as though she would relish having everybody but a saving remnant left out in the cold —or the heat if you prefer—to provide sport for the "saved." (I found out later that Tertullian had looked on that as one of the principal joys of the redeemed; and I remember thinking well, so much for the early church.) And she said her idea of Heaven was a place where you could always keep working with and for the things you loved, to please God, who *loved* you, and ultimately to please and fully "realize" yourself. But this wasn't work as drudgery; instead, as we might say now, it was "doing your own thing" or, as the parable says, using your talents in the perfect freedom which results from serving Him in the way He has ordained for you alone, which is your own life.

And she said she had always resented the "person on business from Porlock" because he came and interrupted Coleridge right in the middle of "Kubla Khan" and then he never was able to finish it and we were thereby denied what must surely have been a wonderful poem. But there wouldn't be any of *that* in Heaven: all the "interrupters," who of course always "meant well" and whose name was indeed legion, would be excluded, along with all the nay-sayers, because of just that: they never said *yes* to anything and maybe that really was the sin against the Holy Ghost, for which there was no forgiveness either in this world or the next. Going to Heaven then didn't mean you would be forced to do without all the good things forever-and-ever-Amen but that you would be able to finish, to perfect them all, both for His glory and your own joy, which was, after all, what the Presbyterian catechism said was the chief end of man. Because she said she thought everybody here had one particular thing to do, one special song to sing, all to glorify God and, as Charles Wesley had written in one of his hymns, thus help to finish then His new Creation. (Was this what the arts and artists were all about?) And if you didn't want to cooperate, He would keep on after you like He did St. Paul, He loved you so much. And what could ever be more exciting if fearful than that, being pursued, even chased by the Hound of Heaven now and forever? It was what we all longed for, though a lot of the time we didn't know it. That was what being "chosen" often meant. Who in the world could ever be bored with that?

But God's greatest compliment to man was that He always let man have the last word. And if some people finally didn't want to go with God, well, He would just reach out and find somebody else. And then those who had refused His invitation would be of all men the most miserable because they would see their situation then for what it really was: *they* would be excluded, left out of it all—all the eating, all the drinking, all the *celebrating*—and by their own desire too. They had said *no*, whereas all the rest had said *yes*, which would be their ultimate joy. For the nay-sayers, however, it would amount to only eternal silence, eternal boredom, Hell itself. But for the rest it would mean being "changed from glory into glory" until they and all creation were finally "lost in wonder, love, and praise"—perhaps for all of us the only real encore possible, ever.

Well, these stories and essays are by no means an autobiography. One would be hard put to "identify" all the characters and events detailed herein, though I am fully aware that, as always, my friends and family will do their best. It is, though, perhaps some sort of record of a journey not unlike that described by Thoreau in the first chapter of *Walden* as what he required of every writer: "a simple and sincere account of his own life, and not merely what he has heard of other men's lives; some such account as he would send to his kindred from a distant land, for if he has lived sincerely, it must have been in a distant land to me."

The Square

Last year when I was home everybody was talking about the new Wal-Mart that had just been opened out on the bypass. It was supposed to be one of their "mega"-sized stores, with practically nothing you couldn't buy; and so one trip would do it all for you. And it would be more convenient and all the rest. Up till now Woodville had gotten along without a mall or anything else, even a McDonald's, but now it looked as though we were about to join the modern world—and with a vengeance. Because lo and behold, McDonald's was putting up one of their "stores," as they liked to call them, right next door to the Wal-Mart parking lot.

Unfortunately, I didn't have time to go out and inspect the premises right then, but I wondered whether Wal-Mart would be following the traditional format, of having a "greeter" at the front door, who was really nothing but a new version of the old-fashioned floor walker but more folksy, just to make you feel more comfortable and of course help to preserve their down-home image. As it turned out, they did indeed acquire a greeter after they got really going some weeks later, and on future visits she would always confuse me with one of my cousins; but after we got that straightened out, she was very helpful with information about what items were stocked where and also her memories of "Mr. Sam" Walton and the time she had had her picture made with him. "He was my darling," she said, after he died.

Her husband had been the fire chief for a good many years, and she herself had once been a beauty operator, so she continued fixing women's hair on the side, even after they moved into the firehouse, which was downtown, just off the Square. And I supposed that lent something to the drama of your weekly shampoo and set: you never knew when the alarm might sound, with the whistle blowing the requisite number of times to indicate what street the fire was on so the volunteer firemen all over town could jump in their cars and get to the scene as quick as the fire engine itself. Unfortunately, however, the firehouse was somewhat on the modest side, with no brass pole coming down from the second floor for any resident firemen to slide down and create a dramatic scene for the beauty parlor, especially if a terrified customer was all connected up to the permanent wave machine and couldn't get out of there in a hurry. But then I decided you couldn't have it all, even in Woodville. And anyhow you could always call "Central" and ask her where the fire was, and she would do her best to provide all the details. And in many ways it was a very comfortable world.

But I had lived in cities for many years, and I knew that sooner or later the old time and place would have to go, even though I had more or less had to agree with one of my city friends who lamented that he had lived to see the "malling" of America. But what I hadn't yet gotten around to was that Wal-Mart and McDonald's and all that went with them sooner or later would spell the end for the Square and as such would doom much of what for me had always stood for Woodville or any other small town. And in due course there would be nobody left down there but bankers and lawyers and the folks that worked in the post office and the courthouse. And everything else would have turned into a ghost town: no ten-cent stores, no picture shows, no "furnishing" stores, like my father and uncle's, where tenants got financed to make their next year's cotton crop.

Of course the through traffic on Highway 51 ("Great Lakes to Gulf") had long since quit going around the Square: that was what the bypass was for. Used to, the Square was the almost literal heart of the town. For one thing, Woodville was built mostly on ridges between ravines, and so all the streets, which followed the ridges, mostly had to go back to the Square to go anywhere else. And so the Square was sort of like a great heart pumping blood (all the traffic) to the town's various extremities. And sooner or later you could see most everybody you knew by just standing on the Square and watching the traffic go by.

And it wasn't just *life* that you could watch either: the presence of death was part of the scene too. Messrs. Waterfield and Hill owned a furniture store on the south side of the Square, but upstairs they had an undertaking establishment. (I think in the old days undertakers and furniture dealers had a natural affinity for each other because somebody had to make the coffins as well as the furniture, and so such dual establishments were quite common on the small-town scene.) And often as not, you would see Waterfield and Hill's hearse backed up to the front of the store, and you knew that some "body" was upstairs being worked on. And somehow it never seemed morbid or depressing—just life and death keeping company, side by side, in the most natural relationship of all.

But they were long gone now, and Woodville had a real funeral "home" just like everybody else—a rather grand old house that had formerly belonged to the town's leading banker before he passed on to his reward. But anyhow everybody said the house had been so easily converted from a private residence into a funeral establishment, it was all right spooky, just like a corpse looking "natural." But whatever the case, I think the Square for most people always stood for life and continuity, the essence of the place, the community itself. And most everything that happened down there was not only of public interest; it was somehow the substance of life itself.

Of course it was not without its own element of color. On Saturdays when I was a little boy, you could see the farmers' wagons (some of them with straight-backed chairs in them, to give the passengers more dignity and comfort) and their mules and horses too, hitched just off the Square in the forerunners of modern-day parking lots. And the Negroes naturally all congregating in their section of the downtown scene they called the Zoo, laughing, talking, visiting with each other. And there would be the throngs, both black and white, collecting in front of the picture show—the New Dixie, where I saw my first movies, seated in my nurse's lap in the Jim Crow gallery. And they would all be impatient for the first show to let out so they could go to the second one. (Most of us in my crowd thought you had to see the whole program—horse opera, Three Stooges comedy, and serial—at least twice to have any standing at all.) And everywhere there would be noise, laughter, life, so much so that later on I came to think of it all in terms of Dr. Johnson's description of the "high tide" of London life along the Strand as one of the great felicities. To see the Square during its finest hour you really needed to be there on Election Day, but of course such occasions were few and far apart. And any day would do when you came right down to it.

There were the drugstores too, all with their soda fountains of course —one of the fountains even christened the "Mattie Maud" for the respective wives of the two owners, another selling that best of all local ice creams, Fortune's "all cream ice cream"—and the ten-cent stores, one of them called the Ben Franklin, presumably to honor one of the Founding Fathers who had always had an eye out for a good bargain. And there were even a couple of "up market" men's and women's stores that catered to the carriage trade that didn't always choose to go to Memphis. And the slogan of the men's emporium was, grandly, "one man understands another," while the ladies' shop, even more ambitious, called itself a "salon." But one of my aunts told my mother, child, not to ever in this world let old Mrs. Harris, who was the boss and manager there, fit a corset on her because she would fit it so tight nobody in her right mind could even *breathe*. And of course my mother always had to have plenty of room because she kept her money inside her brassiere (in a little crocheted bag) when she went to Memphis or some other "big" place which might be dangerous. But it *was* bothersome when she needed to get some money out of there because she always had to retire to the Ladies' Room to carry out the transaction.

The courthouse was naturally the center of the whole thing—not a very "historic" one but a Roosevelt public works edifice erected in the mid-thirties. But I thought it was handsome, with its yellow brick exterior and, in the very center of the first floor—where the north-south and east-west corridors intersected—an inlaid map of the county, highways, country roads, railroad, and all. And in the yard outside there was an enormous cannon, brought up from Fort Pillow, down on the Mississippi, where Forrest's alleged "massacre" had taken place, and now serving as our Civil War monument. Not for us "the little bitty man with the great big gun," so often denigrated by the Yankees as an incarnation of Confederate vanity, but a reality which had once done yeoman service in the fray and as such demanded respect and veneration now from both Blue and Gray alike: no stage property at all.

The yard was also where the old men sat—on benches provided and appropriately so labeled by one of the local lumber companies—smoking, telling tales, playing checkers, even a few of them playing chess, a game I never could understand—and all of them irreverently dismissed by a friend of my mother's, who had dutifully nursed and buried a father and two uncles and all of them as mean and cranky as you could want, as the D.P.'s, which in her context meant not Displaced Persons but Dead Peters.

There was also an ornamental fountain which splashed nearly continuously into a pool around its base, surrounded by red and yellow cannas. And in and out of the whole scene played the squirrels, who lived in the big oak trees nearby and seemed to think it all belonged to them. When we were all quite small, our nurses would sometimes take us and our ice cream cones (brought across from one of the drugstores) to play in the yard; but on the whole, it all seemed too crowded, too busy for us and them too. And so we would usually adjourn to the Methodist Church steps, a couple of blocks away, where we could chase each other around the velvety lawn and play hide-and-seek in and out of the flying buttresses, while the nurses could sit in the late afternoon sun and gossip about both themselves and the white folks for whom they worked.

But back to the Square again. Yes, it was the center of the town's commerce, but other matters were transacted there too—and often matters that were concerned literally with life and death. In those days the doctors' offices were nearly always situated up over the drugstores on the Square—I assume for convenience in case prescriptions had to be prepared and purchased right on the scene. But anybody that had any sense, my mother always said, knew that sick folks didn't have any business climbing the stairs. And, as previously noted, the undertakers were there too; and of course they were the ones who would take you to the hospital in Memphis—in the hearse naturally—if your case required that. And obviously if you died en route or after you got there, they were even more useful still. (It was all quite conveniently arranged if you thought about it.) Then finally just off the Square and right behind my father and uncle's store was the county jail, and you could hear the "jail birds," as we called them, singing nearly any time, from the back door of Drake Brothers. And since they were mostly Negroes, it would be spirituals that we usually heard, full of both joy and grief. It was all of it right there around us too—life and death, Heaven and Hell, the drama of our lives, the drama of the Square.

Well, it took more than Wal-Mart, even coupled with McDonald's, to bring about the modern decline of the Square. We all should have expected it—and perhaps some of us did—when it became apparent that the big trade day (when the farmers came to town) was no longer Saturday but Friday (when the factories paid off). It was really a whole culture that began to go. Wal-Mart was perhaps just the final sign or symbol; it wasn't the cause but the result. And in its own way it too constituted something of a community, though one based not so much on custom as economic necessity, even survival. But where else, we may well ask, does custom, community itself come from? One way or another we must all hang together in this world: no amount of social or technological development can change that, whatever other innovations it brings about. The forms may differ, may undergo mutation in the fullness of time but never the substance, the essence, I believe. And yes, we need each other today as much as we ever did; and no, it is still not good for man to be alone.

Louella and Mr. Kelly

When I was growing up in Woodville, Tennessee, back in the thirties, we lived on Jackson Street, which was also U.S. Highway 51—the Great Lakes to Gulf route, as it was called. And of course it went right round the Square too, with traffic running both ways; and anybody that could negotiate *that*, we always said, ought to be able to drive wherever roads of whatever sort went. And though I've never driven in England (I'm still skittish about the left-handed business), I've nevertheless driven in Italy (Rome and Florence both); and I'll put them up against most anything you can bring out of the woodwork in Woodville or anywhere else. In those days it never occurred to anybody to think of a bypass or routing the highway some distance off the Square, even out on the edge of town. I know U.S. 51, when it reached the next county seat on the way from Woodville to Memphis, did bypass the Square by a couple of blocks and people somehow thought that was scandalous—not advertising the town sufficiently, not giving it enough "notoriety," as they called it. Nobody then ever thought it would be a *nuisance* to keep all traffic, whether local or "through," running round the Square, night and day, seven days a week. But it was all very convenient for us because after they left the Square the Greyhound buses went right by our house, which of course was on the highway to Memphis, and we could just stand at the bottom of our front steps (we lived on a high bank, up from the street) and catch the bus as it came by, then get off there when we returned. The trains of course were more difficult: you naturally had to go down to the depot for that, but that's what you mostly did for long-distance travel in those days and thought nothing of it. Except, that is, for the times you might want to go either east or west. Because everything about Woodville was on a north-south axis, and you could get on the bus or train and go to Memphis or New Orleans or Chicago or St. Louis without batting an eye. But God help you if you wanted to go to Nashville or Knoxville and on "up East," to say nothing of Texas or California or anywhere else "out West." That involved all sorts of shenanigans, like changing trains in St. Louis or Cincinnati, Dallas or El Paso and God knows where else. After all, the Mississippi River was only fifteen miles to our west, so that was obstacle enough in that direction (there were no bridges across the river between Memphis and Cairo in those days—and only one now). And to the East there were the hills and hollows of the Tennessee Valley and nothing much going anywhere else but toward the mountains of East Tennessee. (My father said it was all because of the War and Reconstruction, and that bunch of mountaineers over there didn't ever want to get out of there anyway, and that was certainly all right with him. They were nothing but homemade Yankees anyhow, he said, and it was all quite good enough for them.)

But of course times have changed now, and we can't think of anything *but* bypasses and superhighways, and everything goes *around* the town, never *through* it and nobody knows where he is or is going any more, and geography is a lost cause because we're all either zooming down the interstate at eighty miles an hour or else flying through the air five miles high. And nobody can *see* anything. And finally nobody really knows where he's *at* any more, and it really doesn't matter to him anyhow (one place is just as good as another), so no wonder the world is in the fix it's in. And it all makes you think of Thoreau and the dim view he took of *speed* at the expense of *destination* and *quantity* instead of *quality*.

Well, there's no point in crying over spilt milk: it's our world and we have to make the best of it. And of course we've brought all of it on ourselves and there's no one else to blame. But those were happy times for me, in lots of ways, with the buses running right by our door, the trains chugging through at all hours day or night. And it was all *convenient*. And something else: it was all *personal*. You knew most of the people you were traveling with, from up and down the line; and you even knew the bus drivers and sometimes even the train conductors. And so two of the most important people in my life right then were my nurse, Louella, and the bus driver named Mr. Pat Kelly, who drove the eight o'clock bus down to Memphis in the morning and the five o'clock bus back that afternoon. (It went on up to Paducah, I think.)

In those days nearly everybody had nurses—mostly so they could take care of the children while the mammas did all the work. And indeed, they made that whole world possible. And the same was true of people like Mr. Kelly—always on time and as fixed as the North Star. You could *count* on him, just as you could on Louella. And neither one of them put up with any foolishness. If somebody got on Mr. Kelly's bus three sheets in the wind, he would be cordially asked to leave and if that didn't work, peremptorily escorted off if necessary. And he wasn't having any portable radios or any other kind of noise-makers on board either: you were supposed to act like adults and behave yourself. No bad language either. And he would get you where you were supposed to go, right on time. He was somewhat on the heavy side—not fat but just what we would call stout. And perhaps that made him seem more authoritative. Whatever the case, he made you feel like he could *handle* any situation that came up, just like Louella. And on "his" bus his word was law. Of course in those days the Negroes sat in the back, and one might have thought he would have discriminated against them in matters of conduct as well. But not so: white folks had to toe the line just as carefully. I don't think he really had a high opinion of the human race anyhow, and for him the color of one's skin didn't seem to matter much either way. In that respect you might have said he was thoroughly "democratic."

In any case, Mr. Kelly got to know me and Louella early on, not too long after she came to work for us, when I was about three or four. And it came about something like this. After breakfast every morning my father would drive down to his and my uncle's hardware store in his pickup truck, taking me along for the ride and stopping off at the ice plant to pick up fifty pounds of their product for the drink box at the store. Then he would drive on there (one of the clerks had already opened up) and start replacing yesterday's ice with today's ration and more or less getting ready for the business of the day. And it would be about that time that I would start fidgeting to go home, really fidgeting for Louella, who walked up from her house down in Future City to the store, to pick me up on her way to work. And somehow Mr. Kelly became aware of the daily schedule we were operating on, so he insisted on our riding down Jackson Street on the bus with him, then letting us out right at our front steps. And more than once the neighbors thought we were having big company from way off.

Needless to say, we always took Mr. Kelly's bus when we went to Memphis for the day to shop and naturally came back with him in the afternoon. With him we all felt completely safe from any perils of the road or any obnoxious fellow travelers who might be aboard. And of course Louella would go too, sitting back in the Jim Crow section, and it was she who of course took care of me while my mother did her shopping, naturally eating in the department-store restaurant (but back in the kitchen) when we did and of course naturally accompanied by me, who didn't particularly fancy the white folks out front. And I don't suppose I've ever felt so safe and secure in my life—just as I did when I went with Louella to the Jim Crow balcony of the New Dixie Theater, which was the Woodville picture show, and sat in her lap while we watched everything from Shirley Temple (whom I loathed—because she was always so sweet and brave in the face of adversity) to Mae West (whom I adored because she didn't take anything off anybody and didn't ask favors from anybody either but if you *did* want to go up and see her some time, it was entirely up to you because she could take it or leave it).

Louella and I had some notable adventures on Mr. Kelly's bus now and then, like the time we rode with him, unaccompanied by anybody else (after all if you weren't safe with Mr. Kelly and Louella, you might as well give up the ghost right then and there), down to spend the day with Uncle John, my father's oldest brother who was a Methodist circuit-rider, and his wife, Aunt Estelle, who lived in a very small place called Frog Jump, about halfway between Woodville and Memphis, fifty miles away. And Louella was all excited to see a place she'd never visited before, certainly one with a name like Frog Jump; but when we got there, Aunt Estelle asked her whether she'd mind washing all the dishes that had accumulated for the last few days because she just hadn't gotten around to them yet, she was so busy getting ready for her "expression" recital. (It used to be called "elocution," then in due course "speech," and she always had a right good-sized class of young Methodists learning to recite comic monologues or sad-eyed "musical readings.") Housekeeping just wasn't one of her "long suits," she always said. So anyhow Louella didn't get to see much of Frog Jump, but she said she wouldn't ever forget that day, even if she lived to be as old as Methuselah, because she didn't much think Aunt Estelle had washed any dishes since before Christ. And however you looked at it, it was certainly a historic moment.

My mother always referred to Louella as being "city broke" because she knew how to do when we went to Memphis or some other big place, and she didn't suffer fools gladly either, even if she was black. But she wasn't ever "impudent," just what you might call "independent." (She didn't run any risks; she was just smart without being feisty.) Once when she was called on to give evidence in a lurid divorce trial (people even took their lunches for fear they would miss something!) that involved one of Woodville's leading families, whom she had worked for before she came to us, she was asked what time her mistress usually got in at night when she was down on the Gulf Coast on vacation. And Louella said she didn't know; and when she was asked why not, she replied there were two reasons: she didn't look at the clock and anyhow she didn't figure it was any of her business what time the lady got home. No, my mother always said, you didn't make anything off of Louella.

Well, I don't know what Mr. Kelly would have thought of Louella's adventures in the wider world, but I suspect he would have been on her side all the way: he didn't take anything much off anybody either and he certainly believed in standing up for yourself and those who were your responsibility. But also, like Louella, he had a warm loving heart, though I suspect he would have been very much distressed to hear it. (After all, he was a Southern male WASP—though his name *was* Kelly—and couldn't allow himself to be taken in such deeds too often.) Why, one time when he heard I was sick in bed with the measles, he stopped the Memphis-bound bus right in front of our house and came in to see me. And of course I was embarrassed to death for us both—for him because he was so openly showing affection, big strong man that he was, and for myself for being made the object of such demonstrative behavior and of course also ashamed because I knew I was *enjoying* it.

But in due course it all had to go—the Greyhound buses that drove right past our house, the highway that left us high and dry to become just another quiet neighborhood and moved out on the bypass, and finally Louella and Mr. Kelly both. Louella of course left when I started to school: that was simply one more rite of passage. (I was getting to be a big boy now, and the idea of a *nurse* for me just wouldn't pass muster any more.) I don't remember about Mr. Kelly, but I suspect it all had something to do with the bypass and other "modern improvements." I really couldn't see him driving back and forth, up and down the Memphis highway all day long, more or less by himself, with no friends and neighbors to accompany him and exchange the news with. Now he would just be more or less a kind of salesman, polite and courteous of course but not really the "captain" of his bus, who knew his clientele and took a personal interest in their welfare, some of them commuters whom he saw every day, others who were bound for some far off destination whom he knew he'd never see again—ships passing each other in the night, you might say. More and more we *drove* to Memphis these days, and we hardly ever saw him now.

I heard my mother say once, almost with sadness, that I didn't seem to want to have anything more to do with Mr. Kelly after Louella left us, but I don't think that was it. I suppose, without my knowing it, they had both of them become something too reminiscent of a world I thought should be put behind me: I was growing up now and wanted to put away childish things. And though I knew there would always be a warm place in my heart for them both, I knew I could never *tell* anybody that, least of all the two of them. But I still think of them from time to time—so different yet so very much alike in many ways—and silently thank them for the many gifts they gave me that are with me still today.

Change of Life

When I was twelve years old, my mother began to go through her menopause, which my father and other people of his generation usually referred to as the change of life. And of course, like most of my contemporaries, I had had no sexual instruction from either of my parents —mostly just a lot of misinformation from my schoolmates. And as is usual in such cases, I got the idea that it was all dirty and something to giggle about, while naturally being horrified by the whole thing—something I hardly dared communicate to my buddies, who were probably just as ignorant as I was. Anyhow, when my father began, awkwardly and with obvious embarrassment to try to communicate to me what it was all about, he said merely it was a time when "ladies" quit being "mammas" and began being "women." But not a word about the gynecological facts involved in what it all *meant*.

But then after I was grown, one of my aunts (the wife of one of my uncles), told me that when she began having her periods early in her teens, she had no idea on earth what was happening. And when I asked her if she wasn't absolutely terrified, she said well, no, her girlfriends told her what it was all about. Apparently, it had never occurred to her to ask her mother. But what I found even more horrifying was that it had apparently never occurred to her mother to tell her what to expect when she got to "that age." This was the same mother, by the way, who, when my aunt told her their neighbors across the street, who were Jewish, were going to have their brand new baby boy circumcised, and then asked her what that meant, simply told her to look it up in the dictionary. I don't know whether the South in the forties, the time I'm writing about, was any more prudish than the rest of the country. Certainly, it had always considered such subjects matters of great delicacy, to be handled with great tact and as many ellipses as possible. And I remembered, in reading *Gone with the Wind*, that Margaret Mitchell had observed, in speaking of the antebellum South, that at no time, before or since, had so low a premium been placed on feminine naturalness. But all such anecdotes as I've just related often seemed to me to smack of ostriches with their heads in the sand, indeed pure, almost criminal negligence.

Whatever the case, when my father told me about my mother's condition, I had no idea, really, what it was all about except that she seemed depressed in spirits and extremely anxious most of the time. I do remember waking up in the night once and hearing her crying and my father trying to comfort her. And she told him she wished she was dead and she feared he might "go" before her, and then what on earth would she do? And my father told her to hush or she would wake me. And I remember it was the first time I had ever realized that my parents might have lives that were secret, separate from mine; and I could feel some sort of wall going up between them and me.

But perhaps most frightening of all was the Sunday afternoon, when we were driving out to my uncle's in the country, where my grandfather used to live—a place that had always seemed the most safe and secure of all—where more than one generation of my family had lived, where my uncle and aunt were always at home on Sunday afternoon because all the family expected them to be; they were all so used to going out to see Pa at that time, they continued doing so after his death. *And you could count on it.* And such knowledge of course is the main source of security for any child. Anyhow, not long ago I was driving out on that same road, to my uncle's house: he's long been gone of course but his daughter still lives there in her widowhood. And suddenly I looked about me and in a flash recalled this was where it had happened—my mother's suddenly bursting into tears—wild, hysterical, incomprehensible—on that Sunday afternoon so many years ago. I even remembered what my parents had been talking about moments before: my father's reminiscence of the time some years ago when a young man from down in Mississippi had come acourting a local girl who duly married him but continued to live with her parents because her husband was a traveling salesman and was so often away from home, which nobody in town thought was a good thing.

My father suddenly stopped the car and leaned over and put his arm around her and whispered, "Now hush, Mamma, you don't want to get Sonny all upset. Think of him and remember your duty to the family and all the rest of us. You just can't lose control of yourself this way, and so far you've handled it all so well." But she wailed, "I just can't seem to do it any more, and now what *will* I do? I'm nothing but a millstone around your neck, and I wish I was dead." But my father said, "You'll just have to try harder. You know, all of us are pulling for you, and you have a duty to all of us too. You can do it; I know you can." And then we drove on to my uncle's as though nothing whatever had happened; and by the time we got there, my mother had more or less managed to compose herself and nobody would have known there had been the outburst of a short time before.

But of course I never forgot it, and I suppose it was one of the rites of passage in my young life—my mother, so charming, so bright, all of a sudden seeming to go haywire right in the middle of a fine Sunday afternoon, when she seemed in good health, and looking forward with pleasure to visiting family whom she was very fond of. None of it seemed to make sense, and I couldn't imagine what could be wrong with her. She hadn't seemed to be ill, and she *looked* all right. I was of course terrified and wondered if she might be going to die, like the lady across the street from us had done several years before, leaving two children one of whom was my playmate. Could any loss be more terrible?

So it was that night when my father came into my room when I was getting ready for bed that he told me about "the change" and what it was doing to my mother. And he said I mustn't worry: all ladies went through it and I must be patient with her and it would come out all right. Our family doctor, Dr. Tom Baynes, had said so; and he was in touch with high-powered doctors in Memphis who could tell him what the latest developments in treating this trouble were. And nothing bad was going to happen, but I should keep it all quiet from my schoolmates because they might think it was all a subject for snickering and joking. It was the first time I had ever heard that illness and suffering could be a subject for levity, and I found that knowledge puzzling, not to say appalling. But again, my father never told me why; and I still perhaps hold that against him all these years later. In general, I knew that he was more prudish than my mother, as was the case with many Southern men and their wives; and in my own adulthood I have known a celebrated football coach who, in listing the "bad language" he wouldn't let his team use, called only the initials of the words, all of them familiar obscenities too. But then later on I met his mother, a good stout Methodist; and I got the feeling that there was little you could tell *her* about football or the men who played it either and she had probably washed out a good many mouths with soap in her day.

So the months went on, and on the whole there were few more dramatic outbursts like the one on that dreadful Sunday. But my mother couldn't sleep at night, and more and more she began withdrawing from the friends and family with whom she was—and always had been—so popular. She had always been so amusing, such good company, every-body said—and such a delightful hostess who was a wonderful cook; and now it was as though she wanted to give it all up and stay at home. And at the least sign of any trouble, she would call my father and he would have to come home from the store and try to reason her back into good spirits. And of course she seemed to have less and less time for me, seemed less and less interested in my lessons at school, my progress in studying the piano; and I felt that somehow she was being changed into another person and one I didn't really know or understand.

The one thing that my father was firm about, though, was her bridge club, which had met every other Tuesday since before World War I! And he wouldn't let her quit going to every meeting: he said it was good for her to be forced to put her best foot forward, even if it was only an act. She couldn't just retire from life: that way madness would surely lie. But it got to be more and more of a struggle to persuade her to go every time the club met. She would manage to get through the meetings with no apparent trouble; but when she came home afterwards, she was exhausted from all the effort it had cost her. Different friends tried to cheer her up, telling her about their own experiences in similar circumstances; but her misery didn't want that sort of company. But what did it want? I doubt that she or anybody else ever knew. More and more she became simply withdrawn into herself and seemingly uninterested in so much that had been her life and her loves before. And it was obvious that she was continuing to go downhill.

Finally, Dr. Tom said she would have to be taken to Memphis, where she could be treated by people who specialized in the sort of illness from which she was suffering. There were also hospitals where such people could be treated to the exclusion of all others too. That was the place for her, Dr. Tom said. So that's where she was taken, and she stayed for six weeks with only my father being allowed to see her. It was decided that I shouldn't go: it might upset her too much and might not be very good for me either. And secretly I was glad: I didn't want to see her any more in the state she had been in when she left home—not her old self, not the mother I knew. And I was learning, I now know, what illness could do to people besides afflict them with pain and suffering—how it could isolate them from all those they loved, wrap them entirely in themselves, cut them off from the world about them so they became immured in a kind of living death. Who could want anyone he loved forced to suffer such horrors, such indecencies?

So I stayed with various ones of the aunts and uncles on the weekends when my father went down to Memphis to see her. And to tell the truth, I began to enjoy those weekends, where there was no sickness, no sorrow, no suffering—where everything seemed "normal" and I was back safely in childhood and not forced to take on so much of the world that I felt was way too big for me. But I felt guilty for what seemed like my deserting my mother. Did I want her to stay in the hospital forever if she wasn't going to come back her old self? Would even death itself be preferable to the shadowy existence she had endured as her illness deepened? And such thoughts were terrifying: how could I feel that way about my own mother?

I remember when my father came home on Christmas Eve (I had had to write all our Christmas cards that year) so he could call my mother's Memphis doctor in some privacy, which he did, then burst into tears ("of joy," he said) at the good news the doctor gave him, that my mother would soon be well enough to come home. But I had mixed feelings myself. Did they *know* she would really recover or would she have a relapse? Would we have to be with her all the time, watching for the first signs of such impending trouble? It was a disturbing thought and one I didn't want to dwell on.

I had been making my own adjustment to her being gone very well, I thought. I was getting used to doing my lessons and practicing my piano pieces diligently, with no urging from her or anybody else. And there was no one around to ask questions about whatever I wanted to do, perhaps no one to say "no." And did I, without saying so or facing up to it, really enjoy my new freedom so much that I didn't ever want to return to the old ways? That was a disturbing thought also. And doubly so because it was tinged with guilt. If I really and truly loved my mother, would I be feeling that way? And of course it was something you couldn't *ask* anybody about. And how much would she be changed when she returned? I had been told that some of the treatments she was being given affected the memory, even caused some temporary loss of it; but would it be only that—temporary? Suppose she didn't remember me or her other family and her friends? Would it all be something you would have to make allowances for, for the rest of her life? That was a dreadful possibility. Did something inside me *fear* seeing her again? I was afraid even to think about it.

Finally, a few weeks after Christmas the Memphis doctor told my father that my mother could leave when he came down to see her the next Sunday. And of course he was overjoyed and couldn't wait for the next weekend to come. I was to go spend the weekend with my uncle and aunt out in the country, and he and my mother would stop by there on the way back from Memphis and take me on back to town. Needless to say, it was a day of considerable stress and strain for me—wondering what my mother would be like when she returned, wondering whether we could go on with our lives as we had been, whether she would realize that some things couldn't now be the same as they had been and that I had become something of a "big boy" in her absence, mainly because, I suppose, I had been forced to. And would she accept that? It was all such matters that preyed on my mind that weekend—eager to see my mother again, hoping that she would indeed be restored to her old self, the person I knew and loved, yet somehow fearful that it might not be that way.

So it was with some diffidence that when they drove up into my uncle's driveway I ran out to greet them. But I saw at once that everything was going to be all right. Because my mother spoke up strong and well, in her old voice, like her old self and called out to me, "I'm back— I hope for keeps—and you've turned into a regular *man* while I was away. I certainly can't call you 'Sonny' any more." And then much to my surprise, I found myself bursting into laughter. But then after that I went up and hugged her good and hard.

Raining Cotton

You know, you get involved in some funny things when you live in a small town like Woodville, really just one jump ahead of being out in the country. And I myself always tell folks I'm just one generation from there myself, and I suppose I'd be there still if my father had not decided early on that, with five brothers and two sisters, they would do well simply to *eat* out there (no thought about making money) and the fewer mouths there were to feed, the better it would be for everybody. So along about the time he was nearing twenty, he came into town and went to work for Wilson and Gause Hardware Company and stayed right there for about ten years or so till he was able to go into business for himself—well, along with his youngest brother, my uncle Buford.

But before all that had happened, the First World War had intervened and my grandmother had died (at sixty-two—just worked to death, they all said—and I don't wonder) and Uncle Buford had joined the Navy but never got "across" because the Armistice was signed just before he was about to embark. And then along about that time, my father had begun to court my mother. They had known each other all their lives and came from the same neighborhood out in the country and were kin to lots of the same people but weren't actually kin to each other. (That's why I've always thought that people who grow up in the country or in small towns, especially if they live there all their lives, know more about the inter-connectedness of things, the patterns that underlie the actions of human beings, the *sense* that life quite often makes in spite of itself than those who are city born and bred.)

Anyhow, one thing led to another and they got married and went to keeping house in her old home down on Jackson Street (her parents had both died of the flu in the terrible epidemic in 1918—so devastating that in Woodville they had to make their own coffins because they couldn't get them in fast enough). And so my mother said she had gone right from being a young lady only a couple of years out of high school right into being the mistress of her own house, which of course sounds pretentious except that she and a lot of other women in her generation took them-selves and their respective roles in society just that seriously. (And of course she had one of the finest senses of humor I've ever known.) In any case, she was quite ready to take on her new job, as it were, with one exception: she said her own mother had always turned over most of the cooking to her, after she was grown, while *she* would finish the sewing. And that's why my mother never did much in that line except darn socks and sew on buttons, and she always said it was a good thing I hadn't been born a girl: how on earth would she have managed my clothes? But my father, who was almost as down to earth as she was, said never mind, if that had been the case, the directions would have come with me and in due course she would have *learned*. But of course her cooking more than made up for whatever might have been her deficiencies in the sewing line.

These days, when superior cooking is looked on as a nine-days'-wonder, and people pronounce the word *gourmet* as though it were something at which every knee should bow, I think of my mother and wonder what she would have said. For her, good cooking was just something you *had* and certainly no big deal. And when people ask me now, what sort of cuisine she turned out, I reply "just old-fashioned Southern country cooking," than which anybody who has been properly brought up knows there's nothing better. The ignorant—and the lazy—are puzzled when they come to sort it out. But it's easy, I always say. Mainly it comprises a great respect for seasoning—not in the sense of fiery spices and such but proper gravies and sauces to complement whatever meat you're serving—after the vegetables have been cooked sufficiently, not just par-boiled as in Yankee interpretations. And Southerners aren't any more partial to grease than anybody else, but they do like to highlight their meats with appropriate amounts of such seasoning. They're also, like most artists, great on improvising, with a little pickle juice added here and other condiments there—cooking by ear, you might say.

And it's all easy and relaxed, something that comes naturally and no big deal—as implied once in a comment our next-door neighbor made when she said, when the grandchildren were staying with her, she just turned the skillet handles inside on top of the stove so they wouldn't knock them off when they ran by and never worried about what might happen. (And she was a lady who had at least four or five vegetables from her own garden every day for dinner—always for Southerners in the middle of the day back then—and in the summertime often homemade peach ice cream. And of course *never* any sugar in her corn bread.) But she didn't *sweat* any of it, as we would now say: it was all part of her—or any other woman's—*metier*, her "thing," as the French would say. And I suspect that she would have agreed with my mother, whose worst judgment about another woman was that "she *won't* cook."

But underneath it all, as the firmest of foundations, was an immense respect for food, not just as fuel for the body but as a pleasure and as more than just physical fulfillment to which one could look forward three times a day but quite literally *nourishment* for both body and soul. Few of them, I suppose, would—or could—have put such dedication into words, never *said* it was literally the center of their theology, the common meal; but I don't believe it would have surprised, certainly not shocked them to hear it put that way. Wasn't some such belief, unstated of course, somehow the foundation or rationale of their devotion to the very concept of hospitality that was really at the heart of the *discipline* they practiced? And it *was* for them a discipline, like all the arts; and yes, the genius was in the details. And as I've heard my mother say many times, anything in this world that's good is *trouble*.

It was all, finally, an article of faith, I suppose, and something you took for granted—like manners, like courtesy—something you didn't have to explain or, if you did, it wouldn't really do any good. And of course fundamental to all such was *tact*, the discipline by which you made your thoughts and judgments known but with the least discomfiture for all concerned, the art which concealed its art. And for this my mother was also famous, I've been told. I never in my life heard her—or saw her—lose her temper in public, though what she might say to my father and me behind the scenes when the crisis was past was quite another matter. She would then say things like, "I gave her the worst whipping she ever got simply by smiling at her rudeness and turning the other cheek."

But of course I always wanted to know whether the other person involved had sense enough to know she had been "whipped." And all my life I've felt I could turn the other cheek as well as anybody I knew, mouth closed though teeth might be grinding unheard inside. But I never liked for anybody to think he could get away with something, put one over on me because, after all, I did have sense and, I suppose, enough vanity not to want that underrated. But my mother always observed at such times that people always knew when you had morally bested them, and I always wondered how she could be so positive. I think now her assurance in the matter came from her bone certainty that unless you were mentally defective (in which case the rules might be temporarily suspended) you *knew* what the laws of society, the rules of human behavior and intercourse dictated and there was simply no excuse for your acting otherwise: would *you* want to be treated thus—her version of the Golden Rule, I suppose? And always you got more by just "rising above" such unpleasantness than you ever would by descending to the level of your antagonist. And thus you would emerge "bigger" than your foe, which must always remain your watchword and goal and the knowledge of which was your only reward. And all my life I was forever being urged: "Now don't ever be *little*."

I know now my parents were really, all along, using colloquial versions of those formidable judgments, "magnanimous" and "pusillani-mous," words which still command my respect; but even then, in my uncertainty, I suspected that they somehow meant business and were concepts not to be trifled with. But I still got tired of always having to be the one to "rise above" things. Why didn't the other fellow have to make a similar effort? And how could I be sure that he knew I knew what he was up to and that I was deliberately choosing to be "big"? (After all, I wanted some public recognition of my rectitude.) And when my mother explained that that was why he always remained the "other fellow"—because he *didn't* make the effort, to be "big," that didn't particularly cheer me up either. If only I could have been assured that he did know what he was doing, wasn't really insulting my intelligence, I should have felt a lot better. But no, I had to remain silent as well as moral, and that hurt—and still does, if you want to know the truth, though at my age, I've decided that "rising above" unpleasantness isn't always the answer either. There *are* times when nothing will serve so well as a good kick in the pants.

But I know my mother was basically right in many ways, especially when there was a question of delicacy involved. And this finally brings me to the real subject I intended to write about all along. My mother, for all her tact and delicacy, was about as knowledgeable about folks and the world as anybody I've ever known; and she didn't put more faith in either one of them than she could help. At the same time she knew that you could still "show your raising," as she was always telling me to do, yet make your views on manners and morals known clearly enough: you didn't have to be "ugly" about it, she always said. And that was the way she handled the situation, which all came about like this.

In addition to their hardware store, my father and Uncle Buford also owned the home place, as they called it, the farm all the brothers and sisters had grown up on years ago. But now some of them were dead and some had moved away, so my father and uncle had bought out their interests and now it was theirs alone. It wasn't a large place at all but a one-family, subsistence farm; and I always wondered how they managed to make a living off it. Cotton was of course the money crop, and they raised corn to feed the stock and of course enough vegetables for the family and hogs for the smokehouse and a cow or two for the milk supply. But the main thing of course was cotton: no matter how hard times were, you could always sell that for ready money, however that might be. And in those days people weren't about to quit raising it: some folks even called it "white gold." The two brothers always kept an eagle eye on how the crop was coming along, wondering how many bales they would make this year as compared with last and so on: its success or failure had a lot to do with whether they made a living for the year or not.

In that part of the world then the cotton crop was naturally of the first importance. And there were times when my father and my uncle even bought cotton from the farmers, acting as intermediaries for the big Memphis firms and the gins in such transactions. It was naturally a business not without risk: you could make a "pile" one day and lose your shirt the next, depending on the ups and downs of the market. And there was something else—the greatest, riskiest hazard of all—something called "cotton futures," which those who got involved with frequently were often swallowed up by, like quicksand, and apparently never heard of again. But, thank God, my folks never got into that.

But back to my narrative. Late one fall afternoon, about an hour before sundown, my father thought he would drive out to the home place just to see how things looked before he headed home for supper. The man who farmed the place, on the shares, by the way, was a good tenant and worked hard; so nobody ever thought he needed more than cursory supervision. And they counted on him to keep them fully informed about how things were going with the cotton and all else out there. But not even he, it turned out, could do it all. Because when my father turned off the main road onto the small dirt track that led down to the farm, he saw a car he didn't recognize parked just off the lane, more or less hidden from sight behind some cedar trees from anybody except someone who knew the terrain very well, someone who had business there.

Well, my father, who was not by nature a suspicious man, nevertheless thought this didn't look exactly right; so he parked his car around the bend, where the unexpected visitors couldn't see it and lit out for Mr. Hawkins's house (the tenant), to ask whether he knew anything about what was going on. But all Mr. Hawkins knew was that a couple had been coming out there about once a week at that time of day, but who they were and what they were doing out there he had no notion; but nothing illegal, he would venture, not even disturbing the peace. That was

why he had taken little notice of it. But he now offered to go with my
father down to reconnoiter, which they did, detouring by the nearest rows
of cotton, which my father was pleased to see doing very well—so well,
in fact, that he picked a number of bolls to take home to show my
mother. It looked as though it would be one of the best crops in recent
years.

But when they drew even nearer the car, still screened by the cedars,
it became obvious that the car was not only occupied but acting as venue
to a good deal of activity which was more than mere social conversation.
And furthermore, he recognized the man and woman involved: the county
sheriff and his secretary. He said later he had to think quick: he didn't
want to start a drama right there on the premises. On the other hand, he
wanted to serve some kind of notice that the couple had been observed
there (recognized or not and by whom they would not know); and their
presence was not welcome—no accusations, no threats, you understand,
but a hint clear and unequivocal. So he just idly tossed the cotton bolls
he had picked along the way into the car, which was close enough for
him to do so without undue effort or noise, which might betray his
presence or identity. And he and Mr. Hawkins then left immediately but
not before hearing the man's voice saying, "What the Hell. . . ." and the
woman, with a nervous giggle, exclaiming in some confusion, "Why, it
looks like it's raining cotton!"

Of course my father couldn't wait to tell my mother about the whole
episode, and they both had a good laugh about it. But, my father said,
there was a serious side to it too: you couldn't have public officials
carrying on around the countryside that way. On the other hand, you
didn't want to start a big uproar which would upset the whole county and
really cause more trouble than it was worth. What he had wanted to do
was give the guilty parties something of a scare but not enough to cause
a scandal, something for them—just the two of them—to think about.
And my mother agreed, after she got through laughing, especially about
the woman's remark about the cotton. And she said just let her alone; she
would take care of it, which she did.

Because the next Sunday after church (we were Methodists) she went
up to the sheriff, who was on the Board of Stewards and so naturally,
with his wife, was always there, looking as pious and sanctified as all
get-out, and gave him the "right hand of Christian fellowship" by way of
a conventional Sunday greeting. And they casually discussed the news of
the day, the weather and the crops and so forth until my mother took her

leave but not until after casually remarking, "I understand the cotton crop is going to be much better than usual this year. Why, in some sections of the county, they say it looks like it's been absolutely *raining* cotton." And then she gave him one of her most gracious smiles, and the sheriff looked like he could have gone through an auger hole with plenty of room to spare. But that was the last anybody ever heard about any of that. And the sheriff in due course was reelected, but his secretary sort of disappeared from the scene and no one ever saw his car again out at the home place.

The Clothesline

When my mother and father were married, they went to live in her parents' house on Jackson Street in Woodville. Her parents had been dead for some years, and her only close relative was her brother; and he wanted the family farm. So it was all very amicably arranged, and my mother took the house, and he took the farm. My father was already established in his hardware business—a partnership with his younger brother, and he said he couldn't take on a farm as well. So that was the way it was all settled. The house, which had been rented out since my grandparents' deaths (they died almost one right after the other in the great flu epidemic of 1918) needed a lot of repairs and refurbishment, so that was what they did before they moved in.

Meanwhile they had rooms down the street at Mrs. Stewart's and took their meals at Mrs. Higgins's boarding house. Of course it all sounds somewhat antediluvian now and something like living from hand to mouth, but in those days (back in the early twenties) there wasn't much choice. And of course newlyweds didn't expect to have a complete house and home right after they married then: you worked, you saved, and you waited. And when you could afford it, then you made your move. And I think my parents must have been very cautious in the fixing-up they did do, mainly painting and papering. But they made few structural changes. O, they put a built-in bookcase on one side of the living room fireplace and a window seat on the other, one of their few gestures toward grandeur. But they didn't take out the old cistern that dominated the back porch, and they didn't move the bathroom, which opened out of a tiny hallway, where the telephone was, between the living room and their bedroom. Only years later, after I was in college, did they extend the hallway all the way to the back of the house and do away with the long back porch that had been partially filling in the "L," which constituted something of a "shotgun" design for that part of the house all those years, and thereby give it something of order and symmetry, which it had never had before.

They made a few other efforts at modernizing but nothing too pretentious. One thing was that they cut a door between the dining room and the kitchen. Before that, whatever the weather, hot or cold, you went from one to the other via the back porch (they both opened onto that), which ran the length of the house. And I remember as long as she lived, my mother always spoke of going "up in the house" when she was ready to leave the kitchen for any other room. And I've wondered since then whether that might not have been a holdover from the days when kitchens were often placed in the backyard—completely separate from the house, mainly to avoid the danger of fire. The only other bedroom besides their own was what we always called the guest room, even after I adopted it as my own in childhood, another holdover perhaps from the old days when everybody made a point of having a "spare" room for company even if they weren't expecting a great deal. Years later, after I was grown and they decided to fill in the back-porch "L," they added another bedroom and bath which duly became mine and the "guest room" reverted to its original status. After all, this was still the South, and hospitality wasn't just a word. (I still can't imagine anybody on earth coming to our house any time of the day or night without being given *something* to eat or drink. He might decline the offer, but it was always made. To overlook it would have been considered barbarous.)

But really that was about all they did at first except for buying some new furniture. My father, who was one of seven children, five boys and two girls, had little if any household goods to contribute: there were simply too many others who had a claim on it, furniture and all the rest. And my mother and her brother had had a sale shortly after they lost their parents (or as my mother used to put it, "after our home was broken up," which in my childhood became the most terribly final phrase imaginable). So there was very little of their furniture left. And neither my father nor my mother was inclined to look backward to the old days, at least not at that point. They wanted a new day and a new life, I think, after the sorrows they had recently experienced. (My father's home had also recently been "broken up," with the death of his mother and his younger sister.) And anyway nobody thought anything about old stuff then; in fact, they most of them wouldn't have given *antiques* the time of day. It was just "old furniture," and many of them thought they had entirely too many things left over from the past, too much dead wood, you might say, right that minute. O, there were a few old things that were around, mainly just because they were needed, like the old oak dinner table from my father's family he said they had all grown up fighting around. But there was nothing particularly "fine" about any of it.

But when I was in high school, my mother did decide to start getting together and having refinished as many of the old family pieces as she could—the old secretary that had been her grandfather's and an old linen chest, put together with wooden pegs instead of nails, that had "come over the mountains from North Carolina in an ox cart." But again, they were just things you *had*, things that were "in the family" and not something to go off and *buy* just to show off with and have folks "ooh" and "aah" over. You certainly ought not to abuse them, certainly ought to respect them, the old family things; but finally they were nothing to *your* credit, any more than your ancestors. The real question perhaps was not their distinction, which might rub off on you, but simply whether *you* could be worthy of *them*. And my mother had no more contemptuous dismissal of both folks and furniture which were venerated simply because they had outlived their time than to call them "broken down aristocracy." And as for the D.A.R. and the U.D.C. and all such, well, you could join if you wanted to; but she certainly didn't need any organization to tell her who she was, she said: that was something anybody who was "folks" was born knowing. And it had nothing to do with money and appearances but what was on the inside of you. My father went even further. He said all this foolishness about working on your family tree might reveal some things you'd just as soon not have known: you might find some of your ancestors swinging from branch to branch thereon!

So they moved into the old house, which, I should say, did have a distinguished if somewhat shabby looking exterior—white columns, green shutters and all—and built shortly after the Civil War; but again, they weren't going to spend money they didn't have right then fixing it up. The cosmetics could wait. And then of course after I came along, they always said, well, every extra penny they now had must go towards what I called my "keduation." And in some way even then I think I knew it was just one more restatement of the old adage "Pretty is as pretty does." And more than once I thought, one way or another, I had been hearing that all my life. Why couldn't things be both beautiful *and* real? And why did you always have to have veneered furniture or silver-plated dinner ware instead of *the real thing* that was genuine all the way through? Even then I wanted the real thing, and I recall my increasing respect for such words as "genuine" and "sterling," sayings like "all wool and a yard wide." And I didn't even like to play simplified "arrangements" of the classics when I began taking piano lessons.

My mother did have her mother's Haviland china (dead white with the scalloped gold band around the borders and so delicate you could almost see your hand through it), and after she and my father were married he did "finish out" the place settings for her: she finally had twelve of everything. And in due course she even bought some fine crystal, but she never had much "real" silver. But that didn't seem to bother her at all. It was what went with the dining utensils that counted with her; and she knew she was a first-rate cook—and a real artist too: she was not one to paint by numbers, and yes, the genius was in the details. But I never knew her to use a recipe for anything except some difficult kind of cake or other dessert, some complicated casserole or pudding, some "made" dish. The rest was all tasting and smelling and judging the consistency by inserting a broom straw bent double into the batter, to see whether it was firming up in the right way. And it was a pinch of this and a "season to taste" of that, and any real cook needed no instruction in that.

Of course the worst thing she could say about another woman was that she *wouldn't* cook, and somehow she always managed to make such a failing seem the unforgivable female sin, worse even than adultery. After all, a woman who *wouldn't* cook was repudiating the entire female function. And whatever adultery was, it wasn't that. Once years later in a conversation with the barman at the Ritz Hotel in Paris I found him thoroughly sympathetic to such views: a woman who *wouldn't* cook was "no woman," he said. And I wished my mother had been alive to hear him. Yes, Woodville, Tennessee, and Paris, France, weren't so different after all. And maybe it was the French themselves who put it best: the more things changed, the more they stayed the same.

So I was used to doing without things that were more for "show" than substance and concentrating on the things that had something of value on the "inside." Yes, I wore good clothes, but always they had to be good ones that would last. And since I had no younger brothers to pass them on to, that somehow seemed a waste. But quality always showed, my mother said, and she had rather have a "few good things" than a lot of junk, no matter how elegant it *looked*. And always you had to look neat and clean, but you couldn't spend a lot of time worrying about your looks. If the Lord hadn't intended you to be pretty, well, you just had to live with that and let Him take care of the rest. And anybody that took too much thought about it or placed too much importance on looks wasn't worth worrying about anyhow.

So early on I began to feel somehow that my parents weren't helping me much with my social standing. For one thing, they were older than the parents of all my friends: they didn't marry until "late in life," and by the time I came along they were both middle-aged and, I thought, old and dowdy. And they didn't smoke or drink or dance, like the parents of my friends; and they always kept talking about the future (the last thing a young person ever wants to hear—his favorite word is *now*) and the things that really mattered, the things that would last; but all such things had somehow to be validated by the past too. And somehow with them it was all one: past, present, and future.

Often the old ways, the old times were best but not necessarily so: neither of my parents seemed to have any illusions about that. And my father would sometimes snort, "People are always talking about 'the good old days.' But I can tell you they were often bad old days." But he never said anything more after that, so I could only imagine what he meant. *Fashion* obviously didn't mean anything to him nor did *style*. And keeping up with the Joneses would have been impossible for him to contemplate. In fact, he didn't even seem to think much of that great American word *new*. So what did he go by then? Well, like I said, things that were inherently of value, that would last, and depended neither on the social context nor the world's approval for their worth. I even thought at times it was like my mother's saying "Good clothes are always in style." Like the Bible said, he certainly wasn't carried about by every wind of doctrine.

Of course every year my mother bought one good black dress at Levy's "Ladies Toggery," as it was called, in Memphis, where the sales ladies up on the third floor were always to be found calmly seated beneath the crystal chandeliers in elegant Louis Quinze chairs that might have come from Versailles. (Certainly, the idea of them standing behind a counter would have been unthinkable.) And when a customer did appear, they would graciously rise, pince-nez and "foundation garments" firmly in place, and with the condescension of a Queen Dowager ask whether they could "help." My mother deliberated long and hard before she bought the annual black dress too, but I never knew her to be dissatisfied with it afterwards, certainly not to the point of wanting to return it. Both she and my father knew their own minds, and they did their deliberating beforehand and after that never looked back. I did venture to ask her one time why she always chose black for her "good" dress, and predictably she replied that black was always in good taste, always in style, and of course it would go with *anything*. Also, she added that since she was not a small woman, she didn't want anything that made her look even more of a blot on the landscape than she already was. And black was good for that. As I've already suggested, she was a woman of little vanity and few illusions.

So I thought I knew them, their thoughts and views on manners and morals and most everything else. And I thought they would continue in their appointed ways as long as they lived, and their lives would hold no surprises. But that's where I was wrong, as we so often are when we think we know it all, especially about the past. And more and more the Bible tells it like it is when it says we are fearfully and wonderfully made. But ironically the revelation didn't come until after they were both dead and gone, and then it came from one of the aunts—the one I always called Auntee, who was as much of a realist as my mother ever was, indeed perhaps even more so because she didn't call a spade a spade but more likely, as she said herself, a dirty old shovel. And furthermore she had been married to a widower who had been married twice before and was *old enough to be her father*. So she *knew* about things. And it was she who told me what happened one morning at the breakfast table shortly after my parents were married and, I suppose, hadn't yet finished the work they were doing on the house and weren't really settled in yet. And it was this.

All of a sudden my father seemed to freeze in mid-air with his coffee cup halfway between the table and his mouth as he looked out the kitchen window into the backyard—seeing something out there that was apparently new to him, something he hadn't noticed before. And without saying a word to my mother, he deliberately rose from his chair and just as deliberately walked to the back door, opened it, and stepped down from the porch into the yard and made straight for the clothesline, almost as though he had never seen one before. And very carefully, and again very deliberately, he took it down from the posts to which it was fixed, rolled it up, and brought it into the house and, according to what my mother told my aunt, seemed to stand there with it in his hands as though he were confronting her with some heinous offense (she couldn't imagine what) and said to her, as calmly as if he were making his final pro-nouncement on human behavior and particularly on the married state itself, "If it hadn't been for the washtub and the clothesline, my mother would be alive this day; and I'm not going to have you killing yourself with nothing but drudgery while you're still a young woman. And the first thing I'm going to do tomorrow is get you a wash-woman so you won't ever have to do that. My mother wasn't but sixty-two when she died, and we all thought she was an old woman. Just worked to death was what it was, really. But by God, people don't have to do that now, anymore than they have to die of typhoid fever at twenty-seven, like my younger sister." And he walked over and threw the clothesline in the garbage can, then stalked out the back door to the garage and his pickup truck.

I gather my mother wasn't unduly perturbed by this display of temper: she had seen that before. But she told Auntee she *was* surprised to hear him take the Lord's name in vain, and indeed I never heard him use profanity or a four-letter word in my life. And I wondered what his mother, my grandmother, whom he and all the others adored, would have said. But I thought his reckless language might have been some indication of his affection for her and his fear that something of the same fate might overtake my mother. And she would have understood. Suffice it to say that it was only shortly thereafter that Aunt Georgia Simpson began to do our washing: my father took it by her house down on the railroad cut every Wednesday morning on the way to the store, then picked it up on his way home to supper on Saturday night. And that arrangement went on till well after I left to go off to school.

But I never forgot Auntee's story of how it all came about, how I learned something then about my father and, to some extent, my mother too that I had never known before and how I came to know them in a somewhat different way and thought about them differently even now that they were dead. And I would recollect that, unlike many people, my father never got the giggles when he saw a washing machine almost defiantly sitting on the front porch of some sharecropper's house down in the Mississippi Bottom after TVA came to our county the summer I was twelve. And he would never complain that nobody could cook a ham or bake a coconut cake now as good as my grandmother back in the old days, beloved though she was by them all. And though his father, my grandfather, had been a real live Confederate veteran, he didn't spend much time lamenting the fate of the Lost Cause either. For him I think it was just one more thing you had to put behind you and go on ahead from the present—and the past—into the future, no matter how sad it might be sometimes. And he could even laugh at a photograph of my grandfather and two other old veterans down at our depot all dressed up in their Sunday best, waiting for the train that would take them to the annual Confederate reunion and say he knew those three old men still had stout soldiers' hearts whatever their age because there they were going off to the big city (Birmingham, I think) and all ready to kick up their heels and cut the pigeon's wing and he would bet they didn't have as much as $50 between the three of them right that minute!

Well, in due course I went off to school and fell in with a group of red-hot Southerners, both students and faculty, that spent a lot of time discussing the ways of history and the imminent decline and fall of Western Civilization and always more or less refusing to let the dead bury the dead, Southern or otherwise. And of course enjoying every minute of it too.

For a time I found it all somewhat romantic and glamorous, all their talk of the War and Reconstruction, to say nothing of the antebellum days; but I noticed that their version of it was inclined to be much more deodorized than what I had been brought up on. It was all high constitutional issues too and Technicolor, with little dysentery and no pneumonia. And I thought I might finally have to beg to differ with them, like a real revisionist historian. They didn't have any monopoly on the script and certainly nothing that entitled them to imply that they owned the show and your testimony was but nought—just like saying "you should have seen the garden last year."

After all, there had been my own grandfather, whom I remembered very well; and he had been at Appomattox and had seen General Lee riding down on Traveler to bid his men farewell. And he hadn't particularly distinguished himself in combat either: he ran away from school, to join his older brother, who had already enlisted, and remained a private in the artillery until the very end, when he was "paroled" at Appomattox. And after the war he had emigrated from Virginia to West Tennessee hoping to recoup his failed fortunes, which of course he never did; but he did have the great good fortune to meet and marry my grandmother, whose people, unlike his own, had not been slave owners but did have a small farm, from which they managed to eke out a living, with little help, I gather, from my grandfather, who mostly liked to sit on the front porch and talk about the old days. And more than once I heard my father imply that if it hadn't been for their mother, they would have all starved to death. It was something like this that I longed to tell my new friends, though I wasn't altogether sure what they would make of it. Indeed I wasn't always sure what I thought about it myself.

But I knew this much. History wasn't just something I had "taken up"—another enthusiasm, another sport, like genealogy. I had often had it, the ocular proof, right there in the house with me, in the person of my grandfather, who ate peas with his knife and didn't like to bathe any more often than he could help. And it was all quite literally in my blood. But most of all I wanted to tell them about my father and the clothesline.

It seemed to me somehow that they needed to hear about that more than anything else I could tell them, and I always wondered what they would say.

The Living Room

"Well," my father would say when he and my mother drove past the crowded parking lot of the local funeral home, "I see they've got somebody in the *living room*," which of course always irritated her because that meant they had a *body* out on display in the front part of the house, which was a converted "old colonial home," and yes, in what had been the living room. It had belonged to the Banks family for years till they finally all died off or moved away (the children weren't about to come back to Woodville). And so they sold it off to a new "concern" called a "funeral home," which was an institution gradually taking over the undertaking business.

Of course my mother held no particular brief for the olden time or the Banks family or anything to do with them. She said old Mrs. Banks, the Dowager Duchess of the tribe, you might say, was the bossiest old cat she ever saw in her life: she bossed her husband and her children and the Baptist Church and anything else she could get her hands on. And God only knew what she would say if she knew her former abode was now the funeral headquarters of the community. And indeed I think my mother took some wry pleasure in contemplating the fact. The Bankses were always more show than anything else, she said. Anyhow, Mrs. Banks was gone now, and you didn't have to worry about her anymore.

The form in those days (back in the thirties) was for some enterprising undertaker to find an old house—an imposing one of course—that had come on the market because none of the heirs wanted to live there, then buy it, and turn it into a funeral "home," which nomenclature always made my flesh creep. I just didn't see how you could domesticate death so easily: "home" was the last word I would have thought of, at least as the site for such a business. Of course before that there were "funeral parlors," usually down on the Square or elsewhere in the business district. And they were often owned and operated by furniture dealers. (I suppose it all started out with them making coffins as "furniture" and going on from there.)

Well, everybody said those days were going fast: now people wanted the whole business—at any rate the service itself—transacted away from home and preferably at the funeral home itself if not in the church. But that of course usually depended on how "big" a church member the deceased had been or perhaps whether there had been anything sudden or scandalous about his death—anything that might turn it all into a "big" funeral. In the old days the service had usually been held at the "resi-

dence," as the black-bordered funeral notices distributed to all the places
of business around the Square would put it—along with who the pall-
bearers (both active and honorary) would be and where the "interment"
would duly take place. And so the funeral "home" was the natural answer
to that. And people said places like Waterfield and Hill, the furniture-
store undertakers down on the Square, were on the way out: you had to
move with the times in the funeral business, just like any other.

And so, like I said, some enterprising mortician would buy an old
house—usually a very fine one—and remodel and redecorate it—and turn
it into a funeral home. And the new one in Woodville—the first one most
people around there had ever seen—was moving in on the territory and
would, in due course, do a land office business as they put it. And it was
quite uncanny, people said, how easily the old Banks house lent itself to
the new dispensation: you would have thought it had all been planned as
a funeral establishment from the word *go*. The former living room was
indeed a long drawing room, where the congregation could sit during the
services (always on those folding chairs you could ask to borrow, if they
weren't in use, for family reunions and club meetings). And there was a
connecting sun porch, which was easily turned into a "family" room so
the immediate kin could be secluded in their grief. I think they even had
the dining room, which opened out of the living room behind glass doors,
all lined up as the back-up room in case they had more than one body at
a time to deal with. The coffins and "preparation" all went on upstairs.
And it was all an asset to the community, people said, and particularly at
Christmas time when they had a replica of the "little brown church"
displayed in the front yard, all lit up with Christmas lights and with
Christmas carols all piped into the edifice from the public address system
inside the house. And of course, they made their presence known in all
the local churches with the fans they put in all the pews. They usually
featured Jesus in the Garden on one side and the funeral home's adver-
tisement on the other, where, among other things, they always made a
point of telling you they had a "lady attendant" on their staff—to
preserve the proprieties, I suppose.

Over the years the funeral home became more and more important in
the community, and Waterfield and Hill finally retired from the business,
just sold furniture these days. So when somebody looked knowing and
nodded his head and said, "You know, they've got John Doe"—or
whoever—"up at the funeral home," you didn't have to ask what for. You
knew *he* was the body and the star of the show. And everybody would

say, "Well, I declare . . . ," or even one time when Cousin Rosa Moss went over to see the undertaker's wife (they had an apartment in the back of the house), she was surprised to find that her old friend, Miss Carrie Bond, was the main attraction, only as she put it when she called my mother she said, "I came over to see Mrs. Taylor and I found Miss Carrie Bond here." Like she was still alive or something and just paying an afternoon call. Like I said, it was all very much a community affair: Taylor's establishment was the only one in town and simply in charge of that side of life—or death—in Woodville. And perhaps, little by little, people did begin to think of it as some sort of "home." And thus they were domesticating death there, though they wouldn't have him in their own homes these days. And that was perhaps a credit to the atmosphere the place created—and of course a very wise business stratagem.

I know my uncle Buford, who was very conservative in most of his views, thought the rise of the funeral home had, as he put it, been one of the biggest "improvements" in modern life. (I wonder now what he would have thought of Forest Lawn.) And I used to wonder why he felt that way until I recollected that when he and my father and their brothers had all been growing up out in the country, death had to be dealt with right there on the premises, and perhaps he thought it all too domesticated. You had to come into town and buy the coffin, then prepare the body right there at home and usually hold the services there as well. And it was all immediate and intimate and going on right there in your face and you couldn't get away from it. But the funeral home took all that away and made a professional thing out of it (no real domesticity there), and you didn't have to worry about it beyond selecting the coffin and maybe providing burial clothes for the body.

And I thought this somehow an improvement too—but altogether impersonal, like death was just another business (was it?). But I do know that many older people had a horror in those days of being taken away from home for such purposes: they still wanted the ministrations of family and close friends at such times. And right now I have a very vivid memory of seeing the body of the lady who lived across the street from us arriving from Memphis, where she had had surgery and in due course died. (And they always seemed to do that especially when they had been "rushed to the hospital in the middle of the night," usually for some sort of abdominal operation, like a red-hot appendix or "locked bowels," as an intestinal obstruction was called in those days, which made it sound absolutely final and like the Unpardonable Sin or the Last Judgment.) But anyhow, I was only about five or six and didn't really know what I was seeing—just Waterfield and Hill's big ambulance/hearse (convertible either way) pulled up in front of the house and the driver and another man taking out a stretcher with something on it all covered up under a blue bedspread and carrying it into the house. And I wondered what on earth it was but didn't know until years later that the deceased had said she had a horror of being "prepared" by strangers away from home and they could just come to the house and do it all. And she wanted Waterfield and Hill too and not just some more "brought on" folks. So that's what she got. They said she was yellow as a pumpkin too, so I assume they had their work cut out for them.

Well, little by little Waterfield and Hill were phased out. And so Taylor's Funeral Home took over more and more of the business. But still people were reluctant to make a clean break with the past and still wanted the body brought back home after it had been prepared and their friends could pay their respects right there. They often continued the old custom of sitting up with the body the night before the funeral too.

But then gradually the funeral home became absolutely the center of the whole enterprise, and I don't know now when I've ever heard of anybody's "loved ones" being brought back home to "lie in state," a phrase which always fascinated me when I was little. (It wasn't as though they were royalty or anything like that, so why "in state"?) Now they're kept at the funeral home for the wake, with people socializing right there in the same room with death and not with any disrespect either: it was the time when you usually saw your kinfolks and friends you hadn't seen since the last funeral. But of course if you did go by the "residence" to pay your respects to the immediate family, you found that there had been enough food sent in to feed a regiment, the casserole dishes all bearing the name of the donor on a piece of adhesive tape affixed to the underside for easy identification. And so some things still hung on from the old days despite the attempts to professionalize it all. I had heard that the funeral business was a very lucrative one indeed. After all, they had you, if you were "making the arrangements," when your resistance was low and you weren't able to put up much of a fight against a hard sell.

But it was all still death no matter how you sliced it, whether you spoke of the "living room," where the honoree reposed, or called it "passing away" instead of "dying" and all the other euphemisms. And now we treat the whole business as some sort of anomaly. People don't die at home any more but usually in hospitals and nursing homes. And they don't say much in the way of famous last words either, what with all the drugs they've been given, merciful though that can be. If they do manage to die in their own homes, you usually hear of it thus: "They *found* old Mrs. Harrison this morning." And then usually there is speculation about how long she had been dead and what she had died of and it was all too bad, none of her family there but then that's what often happened when folks lived alone. And they buried her with her glasses on because hardly anybody had ever seen her without them: indeed she didn't really look "natural" otherwise. And of course that was what the death industry was all about now: conflicting views of *nature* and *natural*. And when you said the deceased looked "natural," it really meant anything but that—just prettified and all dressed up "like a country corpse," as they used to say. And when the old and dying *were* secluded in hospitals and nursing homes—away from all the young folks, their children and grandchildren, what sort of impression of life was that in aid of? Instead of having several generations living in one house or even just down the street from one another, you had separation, exile, segregation, all the rest. And death and dying were no longer seen as definers of life and at the center of the drama. A funeral "home" was no substitute for the real thing, just a makeshift in a changing world.

It was not thus in the world that, say, Emily Dickinson wrote about. In a small country town in Massachusetts in the middle of the nineteenth century death was all around you and thoroughly domesticated, not seen as something out of line. And thus her treatment of death often as a familiar friend, even a suitor is nothing "peculiar" or even pathological. Nor is the attitude that he's a household inmate. He is perfectly "natural" but not in the way modern usage would have us believe. And perhaps we do wrong to exclude young people particularly from his presence like some scandal they will be better off not knowing about. *That's* what I call really *unnatural*.

So it was some such conflict, said or understated, which I suppose led to the teasing which went on between my parents about who might be in the "living room." No, it wasn't a "living room" to either one of them now, and my father believed that just as did my mother. Both of them were absolutely down to earth and facers of facts when it came to what life and death were all about. God knows what they would have said about a marquee I recently saw outside a small-town funeral establishment, which blazoned forth for all to see the name of the deceased and the hours of "visitation," like you were going to a movie. Tacky as all get-out, you might say, and making it all sound like yet another roadside attraction. But again it was death as part of the community, part of life, and something your friends and neighbors would want to know about and would feel disappointed, even hurt to miss out on. They would have felt *left out*, just like they would if they didn't get to "view the remains." So perhaps there's something to be said for the rise of the "home" side of the establishment though sad to think it's perhaps due to the erosion of the traditional home and family in our world. And yes, it *is* almost a community center, you might say, though run as a business and a very professional one at that. But we can't have it both ways, really. The "living room" is anything but that now: deep down inside we all know that, despite all the show-casing and window-dressing. And I can hear my father right now snorting and saying, "Just who do they think they're fooling?"

The Time the Bank Failed

I don't know very much about what happened downtown the day the bank failed because I was in school all day long, but that night at the supper table Mamma and Daddy were talking about it. I got the idea that times might be harder; but then they always were hard in a town like Woodville, what with cotton bringing only sixteen cents a pound. It seemed like as long as I could remember people were always talking about how scarce money was. This didn't seem to have anything to do with the Depression that everybody in the newspapers was always talking about; it seemed like farmers always *were* poor, anyhow.

When Mamma and Daddy started talking about the bank, it took me a little time to figure out what was going on. They kept talking about the bank being closed; and, when I asked what that meant, they said it meant that the bank didn't have as much money inside as it was supposed to. Of course, I knew the bank perfectly well. It was across the Square from Drake Brothers' store with a big sign up over the front door that said "Farmers and Merchants Bank." Mr. Bartlett Evans was the president, and I was a little afraid of him because he reminded me of a bulldog. He was real stout, and I thought he always looked mad about something.

Mr. Evans had a daughter named Miss Alice that had been to school at Vassar, and she had even studied awhile at the Sorbonne over in Paris. She was real artistic, and every Christmas at the Presbyterian church she put on the Christmas pageant. The part I liked best was when they had "living pictures." Miss Alice had people posed in a little house with cheese-cloth over the front, and they were supposed to represent a famous picture. Finally, after everybody got posed just right, they would pull back the velvet curtain; and there would be people all dressed up like shepherds and angels and things, and sometimes Mary and the Baby Jesus in the manger. What bothered me was how they could stand still that long. Mamma always said, "Robert, you can't stand still even for one minute," and I wondered how they could stand that still while the choir sang a whole Christmas carol. But last year Miss Alice had married Mr. Harold Beasley, the high school principal, and I wondered if she would keep putting on the Christmas pageants. The day she got married Mr. Evans didn't come back to the bank after dinner, and Daddy said he hadn't ever done that before. Daddy said, "He just hated to think about his little girl getting married, I guess."

The cashier of the Farmers and Merchants Bank was Mr. Sam Chism, and he was the Superintendent of the Baptist Sunday School. Every time we went down to the Baptist church for a wedding or a program of any kind, he would say, "Just think of all those Drakes from out there at Maple Grove that used to be Baptists, and now they're all Methodists. I sure hate to think about all them being lost to the Baptist church." Of course, Pa Drake was the only one that had ever been a Baptist; but he joined the Methodist church because there wasn't any Baptist church out at Maple Grove when he settled there after the Civil War. Mr. Sam never said anything about this when Daddy was with us, but Mamma always smiled and shook her head every time he said it.

Mr. Sam's wife was Miss Mary. And they had six children that I had a hard time keeping straight, and they lived in a big old white house out on the edge of town where the children could all run and holler as much as they wanted to. They were always entertaining official visitors to Woodville—Rotarians and Baptist missionaries and people like that; and it got to be a standing joke that every time they had company it would always be written up in the society notes of the *Barlow County Appeal* that the table was draped with an "imported lace cloth."

But Mr. Sam was always on hand at every function in town; he usually crowned the queen at the beauty revue and gave away the turkey at the Thanksgiving football game. And he did a lot of real kind things, too. He was always getting people into the Baptist Hospital in Memphis when they didn't have any money to pay for it; and he would go to see them while they were there, too. And if they weren't going to get well and maybe had some property, he would help them make out a will. And when anybody died, he was right on hand and always offered to help you get the insurance straightened out. One time he went to see old Mrs. Latham when she was in the hospital. She had just had an operation for hemorrhoids, but he didn't know what she had been operated on for. So he just said, "Well, Mrs. Latham, I know you're glad your operation is behind you." People used to tell that on him and laugh, but they all thought he was a mighty fine man, and they would trust him to do anything. One time Miss Agnes Hall, a friend of Cousin Rosa's that taught school in Woodville, took him $5,000 that she had saved up and just laid it in his hands and said, "Here, Mr. Chism, invest this money for me like you want to." But when she told Cousin Rosa what she had done, Cousin Rosa was horrified and said, "Agnes, how could you?" And Miss Agnes said, "Why, Rosa, I trust him completely. After all, he's Mr. Chism." Cousin Rosa said, "Hmph! I don't want anybody to trust me that much." But that was the way most everybody felt about Mr. Sam. Another time he sent over to Miss Mattie Russell's and asked her to send him her lock-box key because he needed to attend to some of her affairs, and she sent it right over.

But I don't think Mamma was ever so fond of Mr. Sam. She used to say, "Sam Chism always comes slipping around when anybody is in trouble and talks so sweet and strokes your arm and asks if he can do anything for you. I always feel like telling him that if they wanted him, they'd send for him." But then Daddy would say, "Now, Mamma, don't be so hard on folks. Not everybody's perfect like you are." And then she would say, "Thunderation! Everybody knows I mean what I say. And I don't pretend to be anything but what I am." And Daddy always said yes, that was so.

The third man in the bank was Mr. Roger Thurmond, who was younger than either Mr. Evans or Mr. Chism. People said they had trained him in the banking business ever since he got out of high school, and everybody knew he looked up to Mr. Evans just like a father. I didn't know him very well because he never had much to say to folks. He talked like it was costing him money every time he opened his mouth, but I liked Mrs. Thurmond and Betty Ann and Roger Jr. a lot because they played games together just like they were all the same age.

But now, wherever you went, everybody was talking about the bank. All the merchants on the Square and all the people around town were worried because they didn't know whether they had lost any money or not. What they were more upset about, though, was that the bank examiners had let it out that maybe Mr. Evans and Mr. Chism and Mr. Thurmond hadn't just *lost* the money; maybe they had *taken* it. People didn't know what to think, and they didn't know whether to go sit up with Miss Mary and Mr. Sam and the others or to call up and sympathize or what to do. But a few people didn't take any longer than a minute to make up their minds.

The morning when the bank didn't open and the news began to get around town, Mrs. Edgar Rice came stepping across the yard to Cousin Rosa's house next door like putting out fire. Cousin Rosa was fixing to have the house redecorated, and she and Malcolm Watson from the Watson Construction Company were standing up in the living room floor trying to come to terms. Mrs. Rice was a big Baptist, but for some reason she never had liked Mr. Chism; so she prissed in where Cousin Rosa and Malcolm were talking and said, "Well, Rosa, Mr. Rice just phoned from downtown and said the Farmers and Merchants Bank has been closed by the bank examiners, and I'm really not surprised. I've said all along that there was something wrong with Sam Chism."

Cousin Rosa sort of gulped and then said, "O, Maggie, it can't be as bad as all that. You know Sam Chism wouldn't be mixed up in anything crooked. Malcolm, I expect we'd better wait on this business a little while until I find out exactly what's going on and what state our finances are in." She sounded just like she did when one of her first-grade children misbehaved and it made her sad, but after a while she went and called Daddy down at the store.

For the most part, people were so shocked they didn't know *what* to think. Mr. Parker Reynolds next door to us, who had moved to Woodville from over in Arkansas a couple of years before, was terribly hurt over it all. He taught the Men's Bible Class at the Methodist church every now and then, and people said he could make the floweriest speeches you ever heard. He was always going on about things like the golden sunrise in Heaven where there wasn't any night and a mother's tears for her children that were as precious to the Lord as diamonds. One night about a week after the bank failed we were sitting out in the yard with the Reynoldses, and nobody talked about anything else but the bank. Mr. Reynolds said, "I don't see how those Christian men could have done such a thing—taking the money of all those widows and orphans in cold blood. I know I couldn't *ever* have done anything like that." And then he brought his fist down on his other hand, just like he did with the quarterly lesson magazine when he was making a point in Sunday School.

When we went back in the house, Daddy said, "Parker Reynolds doesn't know anything about all this. There's no use getting up on a high horse about it. Those men just made some mistakes that other people have made and are making right now, only they got caught." Mamma didn't say anything; she just raised her eyebrows and pursed her lips, and I could see she was going to talk to Daddy more about it after I had gone to bed.

But a lot of folks were real upset about it all—like Miss Eva Kendrick. Miss Eva was a friend of Cousin Rosa's and a real big Baptist, but she made a lot of money off of lending money to Negroes at ten percent. Cousin Rosa said, "Every time Eva Kendrick gets around me, she starts talking about how awful it was for Mary Chism to take such a prominent part in the Baptist church and do all that expensive entertaining, knowing perfectly well that her husband was little better than a thief. I just told her that maybe Sam didn't really mean to do anything wrong but just got caught where he couldn't help himself and that maybe the way he got his money wasn't much worse than the way some other folks got theirs." And then I could see that she was crying, and I didn't understand why. It seemed to me like she had gotten the best of Miss Eva.

A lot of people were sort of glad about Mr. Evans, I think. He had the reputation of being mighty hard in a business way, and I guess people thought maybe this would pay him back for being so important and sending his daughter away to school up north and having all those trips to Europe and everything. I think some people even tried to go up and sympathize with him, but it seemed like that was the one thing he didn't want. I don't think any of the men around town had ever been very close with him; he was too standoffish, and I think now they were real glad they could feel sorry for him, even if he didn't seem to want them to. But what really surprised everybody was what happened a few days before the trial. Mr. Evans was at home eating his dinner, and all of a sudden he jumped up from the table and ran out and got in his car. He started up the motor and roared down the street like he was going to a fire and lit out down the highway toward the river. Nobody could stop him, and I guess maybe nobody tried to. But when he was going down the bluff into the Mississippi Bottom, he seemed to lose control of the car; and it went right over the bluff and smashed into a big sycamore tree. The car was completely torn up, and he was critically injured, but he didn't die. A lot of people said, "It would have been a blessing if he could have gone on that way. I guess he just couldn't stand to think of all those people he had swindled."

But Mr. Sam didn't seem to be bothered a bit. He stepped around town like there wasn't a thing in the world bothering him, and the next Sunday after the bank failed he was planning to go down to the Baptist church just like he always did. But Brother Yancey, the Baptist preacher, got word that he was coming and called him up and told him maybe he better not come, feeling was so high. Mr. Sam said, "Well, all right if you think it's best, but I'm not afraid to come. And I'm not afraid to meet my Maker face to face right this minute. I haven't done anything wrong." When Cousin Emma heard about that, she said, "Well, I'd be afraid to tempt Providence that way myself, but that sounds just like Sam Chism." Even when they had the trial over at the courthouse and nearly everybody went (nobody could have stayed home that day except a few people like Mamma, who said she wouldn't be seen at such a revolting experience), Mr. Sam didn't seem to be the least bit worried. He even tried to go up and take Miss Mattie Russell by the hand, the way he always did all the old ladies; but she just turned her back on him and marched off.

Everybody felt sorriest of all for Mr. Roger Thurmond. They all said he was a victim of circumstances, and it was too bad about his wife and children. But his own brother, Mr. Stanley Thurmond, had quit speaking to him.

When the trial was finally over, all three of the men were sentenced to several years in a federal penitentiary because some of the money they had taken had been government money. Miss Mary Chism went to live with her married daughter out in Texas, and we heard that she even worked in a department store out there; but everybody else in the men's families stayed right on in Woodville. I used to wonder why they didn't all move away; but, when I asked Mamma, she said, "Well, maybe they can face things better right here in Woodville than they can anywhere else. And wherever they went, this thing would follow them." And Daddy said, "One thing's sure, they can't ever live it down; they'll just have to live it out."

Several months after the bank failed we were all sitting up on Cousin Rosa and Cousin Emma's porch one night, and somebody began talking about the bank. A new bank had been started by this time, but a lot of people were saying that they didn't want to put their money in it; after all, it was in the same building as the other one and some of the same people were running it. But, for the most part, you didn't hear as much about the old bank as you used to, except for things like that Miss Mattie Russell had had to rent out part of her house because she lost some of her money in the bank. And several boys and girls in high school weren't going to be able to go to college.

Daddy was talking and he said, "You know, Frank Patterson was in the store today and started talking about Bartlett Evans again. You know, he had lent him $10,000; and, of course, he never got any of it back. And it's just about to kill him, he loves money so well. He can hardly talk about anything else. But I told him he could afford to lose it as easily as anybody in town. I just told him he ought to be thankful he hadn't lost any more than he had and that he hadn't done anything for his family to be ashamed of. But you can't reason with a fellow like that. I reckon he thinks they're making shrouds with pockets in them now so he can really take it with him when he goes."

Everybody laughed, and then nobody said anything for awhile. Finally Cousin Emma said, "You know, Mr. Rice next door said the worst thing about a thing like this is that it makes you lose faith in human nature." Somebody said yes, that was so; but Mamma just shook her head and said, "Edgar Rice ought to know more about human nature than that."

Then everybody was quiet for a long time, and I could tell that they were thinking about the bank and all those men mixed up with it and how they felt toward them. Then Cousin Rosa said, "You know, they say that Sam Chism is really coming back to Woodville after he gets out." And then I remembered some new words I had learned and thought this might be a good opportunity to use them, so I spoke up and said, "Why, if they ever came back here, they would be *ostracized*. They're nothing but *hypocrites*." Cousin Emma smiled at me; but Mamma looked at me right straight and said, "Hush, Robert."

The Methodist Church, the Democratic Party, and the St. Louis Cardinals

The day my father died (he had a heart attack and literally dropped dead at the breakfast table) one of his oldest friends came up to me—we were standing in the back hall of our house, just after his body had been removed and before anybody but the nearest neighbors and intimate friends had arrived on the scene—and with tears in his eyes he took my hand and said, "You know, after you and your mother, your daddy loved three things in this world: the Methodist Church, the Democratic Party, and the St. Louis Cardinals." And I said yes, that was about right, though I didn't think I had ever thought of it that way before. And though that's all been nearly forty years ago, I've thought about it off and on ever since then—what it told me about my father and perhaps even what it told me about myself.

And I suppose the main thing was that in all his commitments he was nothing if not *loyal* and forever true to his own. Of course it could all have been different. Pa Drake, his father, had come out to Tennessee after the War from Powhatan County, Virginia, where he had been a Baptist— at the Mt. Moriah Baptist Church in Ballsville—and met my grandmother, who was a Methodist; and because of that and also because there was not a Baptist church in the community where they settled—Maple Grove, it was called—he just turned in and joined the Methodist church after he married and never thought any more about it. But the Virginia relatives didn't much like it and of course people in Woodville, where I was born and grew up, three miles from Maple Grove, took note of it too.

I remember one time when we went to a Christmas program down at the Baptist church, Mr. Sam Chism, who always presided over all the functions down there (he was Sunday School Superintendent for years and was on hand just about every time there was a crack in the church door) said to my mother, as he handed her a program, "Just to think of all those Drakes"—Pa and Grandma had seven children, five boys and two girls—"lost forever to the Baptist Church and now turned into *dry-cleaning* Methodists!" And of course I didn't know what he meant, but my mother whispered to me that that was just a Baptist way of throwing off on the Methodists, who didn't baptize by immersion but just sprinkled you instead. But I could tell she didn't much care for Mr. Sam's sense of humor because she just nodded to him but didn't smile. And she explained to me afterwards that *she* wasn't much of a *denominationalist* but what difference did that make when other people were so hipped on the subject? And I wasn't sure—right then at age eight—just what that meant; but I gathered that she thought folks had better be left alone to please themselves in such matters and whatever they did about it wasn't anybody else's business. (On the whole, she was a great believer in live-and-let-live where most things were concerned, just as long as you didn't send her the bill afterwards.)

So anyhow that was why we were all Methodists; and Daddy's oldest brother, Uncle John, was a Methodist preacher. And even now I can still hear him at the Communion service reciting the Prayer of Humble Access —"We do not presume to come to this Thy table, O merciful Lord, trusting in our own righteousness but in Thy manifold and great mercies . . ." And even now it still brings tears to my eyes, to think of grace so freely given and so freely received. But they weren't *fanatics* about it, just mighty glad they had been "included," like it said in the old hymn ("When the Lord said whosoever, He included me . . ."), like it was all a big party. And one time I even heard Daddy say *why not* since the New Testament was full of parties and eating and drinking and *everybody* was invited (*amazing* grace!) and the only thing that could keep you out was if you just didn't choose to go. It was all strictly up to you. And that was what salvation was all about and maybe nobody ever got *sent* to Hell, which was just an idea invented by all the sanctimonious folks to make them proud of being good and (they hoped) able to look down on all the folks left outside, which of course was the real meaning of Hell. And no, he wasn't a *denominationalist* either.

In a way it was all like Uncle John and his camera. He had been taking pictures of all the family and everybody else that would stand still since the Year One. (When he was a young man, he had fixed up a dark room out in the smokehouse; and that was the beginning of the whole business.) And every time we went to visit him and Aunt Estelle, especially at Christmas when we had five big dinners—one at each brother's house—we all had to stand outside on the front steps while he disappeared under the black hood for what seemed an hour getting everything adjusted while we all stood there freezing to death. And if there weren't enough family to fill up the picture, he would go call the neighbors to come and be part of it too, almost like it said about going out into the highways and byways and *compelling* them to come in: he wanted a full house; and he wanted to include everybody, just like at

Communion, which was the greatest meal, maybe even the greatest party of all.

Well, that was more or less the way Daddy felt about the Methodist Church, which of course in those days was named the Methodist Episcopal Church, South. And of course it was called that because it had broken off from the Church of England because John Wesley had begun to put more "method," more "activity and zeal" (which was a section of the Methodist Hymnal containing the more up and at 'em songs I always liked), into things than they could take. And so they turned him out of the churches, but he went and preached in the fields and said the whole world was his parish and why should the Devil have all the good tunes; so Methodists became great singers and weren't ashamed to be heard making a joyful noise most anytime, most anywhere, to say nothing of shouting, for which they became notorious. (But the Christian religion, by its very nature, always had to be something of a scandal, Daddy said. Didn't people understand that?) And anyhow it was all done out of joy, not fear. And yes, death and judgment were real but that was God's business and not yours. And I have seen my father and the other brothers literally "full" after an affecting sermon, quietly weeping for joy at the Good News. And I would think of Wesley, sitting "very unwillingly" at the "society" in Aldersgate, where "one was reading Luther's preface to the Epistle to the Romans" and "about a quarter before nine" feeling his heart "strangely warmed."

Of course it was not all without spot or wrinkle. My father died lamenting that the northern and southern branches of the church had been reunited in 1939, after which it became known as simply "The Methodist Church." I believe he thought the deletion of the word "Episcopal" as well as the word "South" somehow compromised its orthodoxy. O yes, he knew that the "South" had been added after the split in the denomination over slavery; and yes, Pa Drake's family back in Virginia had been slaveholders. But in his view the farther back the Church's roots went in time and place, the more "catholic" it stayed. (I well remember the time when he explained to me that the word "catholic" in the Apostles' Creed had nothing to do with the Pope.) And I suppose that if there ever was such a thing as a "high church" Methodist, he was one. Incidentally, such beliefs didn't keep him from saying maybe it was too bad the Methodists had given up shouting but the thing was that now they were getting so up in the world, so far above their raising, they would probably have you arrested and thrown out if you commenced to do that during the service. But when you quit preaching Christ crucified, he said, you might as well shut the doors and go out of business. And it goes without saying that he was unhappy about substituting "Church School" for "Sunday School" and "District Superintendent" for "Presiding Elder." But anyway, he said, they couldn't give up the title of "Bishop" because of course that was what Methodism was all about. Whether the concept of apostolic succession ever had anything to do with this I don't know: as a Methodist he may even have been ignorant of the term. But *bishops* seemed to legitimize whatever was authentic and valid in the church for him, and he stood by his allegiance to them. But of course nobody ought to ever try to get above his raising, he said. And he had seen it happen time and again: when perfectly good Methodists from out in the country got to making a little money, nothing would do but they had to up and move into town, start voting Republican, and join the Episcopal Church.

Well, some people might say that, among my father's prime loyalties, it was a long way from the Methodist Church to the Democratic Party, much less the St. Louis Cardinals. But I suspect he would have begged to differ. Because again, it was homefolks you were dealing with and he was always local and always loyal. And both institutions had been hallowed by history and long commitment. The Democrats were the party of the South, and that was enough said right there. My father was anything but an unreconstructed fire-eater, but he did believe in the Lost Cause, though he was willing to concede that the dead had better bury the dead. (Not for nothing had Pa Drake been at Appomattox, the last surviving veteran in our county; and when he died, the Memphis *Commercial Appeal* had come to cover his funeral.) And in general he believed in other "lost" things too: success in this world was not something he took much stock in.

Not that he was indifferent to prosperity and the other good things, but on the whole it had not come very nigh him. He was very proud—and deservedly so—that he had made and saved enough money to send me to school without my ever having to work or borrow myself. And his great delight was to tell me that it was all coming to me "free." And I was to have all the education he had never had. (He was never prouder than on the day when he could first call me "Doctor." And he loved to take guests into my room to show them all my diplomas framed and hanging on the wall, always taking especial pride to point out the Ph.D. diploma from Yale as "the Big Boy.")

But on the whole, I think he would have agreed with the historian C. Vann Woodward that the South was uniquely familiar with the concept of failure and with the word "no"—the only part of our country before Vietnam to know defeat and failure. That tragic conflict has caused some revision in the prevailing American myth of exclusive sanctity and consequent success; but even today most Americans still feel, one way or another, that the frontier is always a valid option—and as real as the green light at the end of Daisy's pier ever was for Jay Gatsby and the "GTT" chalked on a man's barn, which signified that he had pulled up stakes and lit out, in the middle of the night if necessary, to try his luck in Texas. By and large, most Americans still think they can always *move on*. But it has, on the whole, been otherwise with Southerners, for whom the past has remained inescapable, a demonstrable *fact* and still very much alive in the present.

Well, it was something like this that the Democratic Party stood for, for people like my father: a reminder of their loss and a defender of their present and, they hoped, an earnest of the future, after the Republican bankers and brokers had been expelled from the body politic. Not for nothing had Daddy heard William Jennings Bryan speak once, and not for nothing did he remember F.D.R.'s promise when he took office to move the Treasury back to Washington and away from Andrew Mellon and Wall Street. And there was even more drama in the situation generated by the fact that Tennessee was a divided state, with our own "grand division" in the west solidly Democratic and virtually an adjunct of northern Mississippi and East Tennessee still "loyalist," as it had been before and during the War, and staunchly Republican. And as long as he lived, my father could never mention that part of the state without adding "There're just *lots* of Republicans up there," as if they were just so many vermin; and you could have all the mountains and "scenery" you wanted, he said, there was just nothing like that good old Mississippi Bottomland, where you could raise the best cotton in the world. But now I've taught for thirty years at the state university in Knoxville, indeed lived there the greatest part of my life; and I wonder what he would say.

In some cases he mellowed with the years, as he did about my joining the Episcopal Church. He thought, as I did, that the Methodists were forsaking their birthright in some ways when they ceased to proclaim the Good News as much as they did the Social Gospel. (Ironically, the Epis-

copal Church has seemed to be going in something of the same direction
—jazzing up the Prayer Book and exchanging the "peace" all over the
place; and you can now hug and kiss perfect strangers in Westminster
Abbey. But of course Anglicans ought to know better: it's not in them to
be folksy and they ought to leave that for people who were born to it.)
But about matters political he seemed more unyielding. My uncle who
was his business partner told me long after his death that Daddy was the
only other man besides Harry Truman who said all along that Truman
was going to win the election in 1948: that's how loyal—or prescient—he
was. And of course he didn't vote for the Roman Catholic Al Smith but,
as he put it, couldn't "betray his party" and vote for Herbert Hoover
either. Faithful unto death would be putting it mildly.

So where now do the St. Louis Cardinals fit into all this? Perhaps it's
a little difficult to say except that my father loved the game of baseball
(he thought it more gentlemanly than football and the players of higher
calibre) and naturally favored whatever big-league team was close to
home. Because that's finally what many of his loyalties came down
to—home and where he felt he belonged. And St. Louis was less than
three hundred miles away. And it *was* on the verge of the South. (After
all, the "Boot Heel" of Missouri—usually Southern in its sympathies—lay
just across the Mississippi from northwest Tennessee; and the folks over
there didn't sound much different from us when they talked.) So the
"Cards," as they were called, were adopted as somehow ours and thus
worthy of loyalty and support. And like all such fans in our part of the
world, my father would listen faithfully when the "Cards" games were
broadcast and, when I was a boy, regale me with stories of the old days
when Dizzy Dean and the Gas House Gang were riding high and up to
all sorts of fun and games whether in the clubhouse or on the field. And
of course as he sat there on the front porch listening in the summertime,
all rared back in his rocking chair, a coal scuttle beside him so he would
have somewhere to spit when he smoked his big cigar (the "Flor de
Melba" brand named for the opera singer), he would proceed to give
them advice about what plays they should use and commiserate with
them when the stratagems didn't work but also upbraid them when they
erred through stupidity or sloth. And thus they became more or less a living presence right there in our house, and he seemed to know them all as
intimates.

The strange thing was that somehow he seemed to take a greater interest in *hearing* their games than in *seeing* them. It was as though he had rather let his imagination take over and he could then write his own ticket, in some way even be part of the game himself rather than being held down to the bare facts by the ocular proof. It was simply more fun for him, I think. And when he went to St. Louis, as he had to do from time to time on business, he made no particular effort to see the Cards play. And he died before the games were so widely televised as they are today. Now that it takes only a little more than three hours on the inter-state to drive from West Tennessee to the stadium in St. Louis, I wonder whether it would be any sort of temptation for him to go. But on the whole, I think not: where his loyalties were concerned, he never seemed to require demonstration. (". . . blessed are they that have not seen, and yet have believed.") And anybody but a fool ought to know that the homefolks wouldn't let you down, whether in church, on the speakers' platform, or on the baseball field. You didn't have to keep *checking up* on them: that would have been almost like spying. In any case, they would surely give you the best they were capable of right then and there. And he might even have gone on to add that the Kingdom of God cometh not with observation.

All this of course was before the million-dollar salaries, the gilt-edged contracts, and the high-powered agents of today—all signifying perhaps the passing of a sport and the diminution of a commitment, what had perhaps already been foreshadowed in the Black Sox scandal years ago. But for Daddy the prime requisites remained unchanged: duty, devotion, faith. And that was all you could ask of any man in any walk of life, wherever his home, whatever his calling. That things sometimes went wrong, that men could make mistakes, even where their nearest and dearest were concerned was beside the point: as far as they were able, they had kept the faith like workmen that needed not to be ashamed. And as such they had had their reward. And I think now that that was what the old friend of my father's was trying to tell me about him the day of his death.

The Legacy

That morning when we got to my uncle's, the backyard was full of cars, some I didn't even recognize because they were from out of state. His wife, my aunt, had died after a very short illness two days before; and I hadn't been able to bring myself to enter the house since then. But I had heard all about everything that was going on over there because my father had hardly left my uncle's side the whole time: my uncle was seven years younger than he and thus his baby brother. And in many ways, my father still regarded him as a little boy; indeed, he called me by my uncle's name half the time, something I hadn't always appreciated until my mother had explained that it didn't mean that my father loved me any the less: my uncle and I were both his children, to his way of thinking, and thus equally precious. You couldn't imagine anybody having a favorite *child* now, could you, she wanted to know. But since I had no brothers and sisters myself, I wasn't sure about that either.

What my uncle ever thought of this confusion of names on my father's part, I never knew because he never said. Indeed, he never really *said* much of anything; my father did most of the talking in their business (they owned a hardware store) and in their personal relationship, I believe. (They had never had a cross word either, my mother always said.) When my uncle did speak, it was usually simply as a footnote or an emendation to something my father had said. And for the most part, this was true in his dealings with me, at least until I was an adolescent.

I remember once hearing him speak—and I thought with some approval—of old Dr. Steele, who had healed the sick and raised the dead—or at any rate presided over the births and deaths—of several generations all over our county years ago and in the process amassed a considerable fortune in money and land. But he never *said* much. And my mother said that was true: Dr. Steele would come and look at you and watch the progress of your ailment and you could die or get well or be resurrected but Dr. Steele hadn't said yet what was the matter with you or whether you would recover or anything else. But my uncle said Dr. Steele has gotten rich by not talking.

I suspect now, of course, that my uncle was jealous of me; and why shouldn't he have been? My father didn't marry until late in the day, and he was already middle-aged when I was born. And there was my uncle, who, all these years, in a big family (five boys and two girls) had been my father's favorite, his own little boy, you might say, now abandoned for a child of my father's own. So I suppose it was natural for him to resent me. But then I couldn't *help* being there either.

Of course my uncle wasn't abandoned: the mere thought would have horrified my father. But I knew that he never seemed to mind taking me down a peg or two, never seemed to mind deflating me when I was flying too high, or he thought, getting above myself. (He viewed my childhood enthusiasm for the movies and my later delight in opera with wry amusement: he said if I didn't watch out, I would begin to sound like a "Hollywood product" when I talked and look like a "Dago singer" when I gestured with my hands.) And when I was still older, especially after I went off to school, he would always begin with, "Now here's something you ought to know that your Daddy probably hasn't told you . . ." And it would all suggest that my father was somehow mistakenly shielding me from the harsh facts of life, especially where money was concerned: perhaps he thought I was going to be something of a prodigal. But he, my uncle—the corrector, the reprover—was going to set both me and the record straight. (He never ceased to remind me that such limited success as he and my father had achieved in their business was all their own doing: "We had to start from scratch, with nobody to help us," he would say, "and what we've got, well, it's just what we've made ourselves.") Finally, there would be, "Of course, I never had all the opportunities you've had. Do you know that I always wanted to be a doctor, but where was a poor country boy like me going to get the money for that back then?" Of course it was all my own fault anyhow, he implied—to have had so much *done* for me. (I don't remember his ever using the word "spoiled" at such times, but I always felt it somewhere near, hovering unstated in the air.) But then I remember that Daddy was supposed to have quit school to let him go, and I wondered whether he had forgotten that. And I sometimes wondered just how badly he had wanted to be a doctor anyway.

There was a time, after I got to be grown, when it all really used to get me down. When somebody lends you some money, you can repay the loan with interest, and the debt is cancelled. But a *moral* obligation, well, that's almost impossible to pay back. Sometimes, even after my uncle's death (and many years after my father and all the rest were gone) and after I had gained some small recognition in the world, I wondered even then what he would say if I could call him back from the grave and ask him, "Are you satisfied *now*?" But of course there's no profit in such speculation: indeed, that's one reason you write, to try to lay such ghosts.

Of course I would have given anything in the world for some sort of outward sign of affection from my uncle, but it never came. I even heard him speak once—I thought perhaps with some pride too—of not being a naturally "demonstrative" man; some things just didn't need to be said, he added. And indeed, the only time I ever saw him "lose control of himself," which is to say break down and cry, was the day my father died, and then it was all over in a minute. But always I looked up to him as a kind of second father (that's what he really was, Daddy always said) and wished we could be closer. As a little boy, I know it was all I could do— prompted by my father of course—to work myself up to asking my uncle for a nickel. You just didn't *ask* him for things; somehow I already knew that even then. And when I was much older, my mother told me that, where business was concerned, my uncle was a much "harder" man than my father, much more likely to say "no." Of course, my father never saw the distance between my uncle and me: in his eyes, my uncle could do no wrong. (Once when a customer ventured to doubt my uncle's word about his account—he kept the store's books—my father reached for one of the axes on display nearby and told him to get out of there and never come back!) But the distance was there, and of course it would only widen with time.

My aunt, of course, made all the difference. Warm, outgoing, really loving, one of a family of great charmers, she was easily the most popular woman in town, my father always said; and I simply adored her. She had taught school for many years and also directed the Methodist choir, and she knew everybody in the county. But the main thing for us was her affection for my uncle: "she's absolutely wild about him" my mother always said. (But even then I remember thinking she never said how he felt about her.) They had no children, which I always thought too bad; my aunt would have made a wonderful mother, I imagined, and perhaps my uncle would have been warmed and liberalized by parenthood.

But now my aunt was dead, after only a short illness too. She had never been very strong, I gather; and she couldn't ever say no to anybody who asked her to sing at a wedding or a funeral or take on yet another volunteer job. (She always got called on to arrange the music for all the home talent shows—the blackface minstrels, the beauty revues, and such like.) And I remember hearing my mother say that really, she "just lived on excitement." One time I even saw her dance a jig on the front porch for sheer joy when an old friend she hadn't seen in a long time arrived from Memphis for a visit. Finally, I suppose, it must all have caught up with her; but she had always said she had rather wear out than rust out, according to my mother. And now I was simply devastated. I was only thirteen, and it was my first real grief. My grandfather had died several years before; but he was a very old man, and I was afraid of him because of his great age and his big walrus mustache, and so he didn't count. But my aunt was only middle-aged: she had no business to go and die like that. But she had, and my uncle was left all alone now, a widower.

And I think that was probably the reason I didn't go over to their house after my aunt had died, not until the morning of the funeral: I didn't want to face him. He was such a restrained, quiet man—except for his sardonic wit, what everybody called his "dry" humor, which had sometimes been aimed, uncomfortably, at me—and so different in that way from my father, that I dreaded seeing him in the throes of raw grief. Surely he would be "demonstrative" now. On the other hand, I may have been fearful that he wouldn't appear grieved enough. My father, of course, could not mention my aunt now without tears. But perhaps my uncle was being his usual undemonstrative self. How could anybody know *what* he was feeling? And I remembered he said Dr. Steele had gotten rich by not talking.

So I had stayed away until then, but of course I had to go to the funeral. My mother was unwell, so I went all alone with my father. And shortly before we were to leave for the church, my uncle's small house was bursting with people, our family and my aunt's (some from out of town, even out of state) and a few close friends. We had come in through the kitchen: and of course there was enough food for an army there—sent in by friends, as is the case in small towns in a time of sorrow. But there was little time to say more than a few words to anybody now because it was almost time to start for the church.

However, I did notice one thing. There was a line of people all waiting to go into my aunt and uncle's bedroom, looking very solemn and speaking only in whispers. And I wondered what it was all about. Then suddenly I knew: they were going in to have "the last look" at my aunt before the coffin was closed. And then for the first time the finality of her death—maybe all deaths—laid hold of me: she was gone, and I would never see her again except as a corpse, *something to be looked at*, on display. And people would say—or not say—how "natural" she lookeded. And I couldn't take that, so I signaled to my father that I would wait for him in the kitchen. The line continued to move into the bedroom, but my tears were coming too fast now for me to notice anything else until

I heard a woman's soft voice in the distance. And then I raised my eyes; and by some curious freak I was looking right up into the mirror on the dresser in the bedroom where my aunt's body was lying, and I could see reflected there the people passing by her coffin but not the coffin itself, only its raised lid. And then I saw what I had heard. My aunt's sister had her arm around my uncle's shoulder, and she was supporting him as he bent over to kiss my aunt goodbye. She talked very quietly to him, and of course I couldn't hear what she was saying but I could imagine. She didn't let him linger, though, and she raised him back up to an upright position. And that was all: the little scene was over.

But I was shattered. It was as though I had intruded on the most private moment in the world for my aunt and uncle, more private, much more so even that the act of making love. I wasn't even sure I had ever seen him kiss her before; and now this was the end of the affair for them, the most intimate relationship possible between two humans, and the finishing off of what I could only assume had been their great happiness. And I felt that neither I nor anybody else had any right to be present at so sacred a moment: I was shocked and embarrassed both for them, my aunt and uncle, and for us, who had been the unintentional spectators of the scene. And indeed, so strong was its effect on me that I've never spoken or written of it to a living soul until now. I had intended to walk with my father in the procession into the church, but I saw now that he was going to walk beside my uncle (with my aunt's sister on the other side). And I couldn't bear to be so near the remnant of the intimacy I had seen so recently exposed; so I faded into the background, to walk with one of my cousins. And in that order we went on to the funeral.

That's been over forty years ago, but that scene has stayed with me ever since—indelibly etched in my memory. What had my uncle shown there, in that last kiss? Warmth, affection I had never known he possessed? Or had he merely been forced into the act by my aunt's sister, a sentimental gesture and that only? Was there some sort of key to the puzzle of his character there if only I had known how to read it? Even today I don't know; and it's been such a private matter I've carried in my heart all these years (between my uncle and my aunt and me, really), I've never been able to tell anybody about it. Of course, there were other spectators to the kiss (and I had seen it only second-hand, as it were, in the mirror); but I didn't think any of them knew what I knew about my uncle's seeming coldness, my aunt's great love for him, and my own sense of bafflement about what their relationship must have been.

And today I still don't know what to make of that tableau, which flares up before me from time to time, sometimes almost in a white heat, to pose the same questions, not only about the three of us, my aunt and uncle and myself, but maybe even about human relationships in general. Had my uncle been as "wild" about my aunt as she had been about him? And if he could love, why couldn't he show it while you were alive? Couldn't he say "I love you" to *somebody*? (Were some people simply that way? And whom were they getting back at anyhow?)

He loved my father: I felt certain about that. I remembered once seeing him dash out of the store, my father's raincoat in his hand, and, without saying a word, place it around my father's shoulders as, oblivious of a sudden shower, he wrestled with a refrigerator he and one of the clerks were preparing to deliver to a customer in the store's pickup truck. Then, just as quickly, my uncle returned to the store; and my father went right on with his work, both of them still silent. And of course no words were needed: action said it all. But did my uncle also somehow resent that warmth which so characterized my father in his relationships, perhaps resent my father's still treating him like a little boy? Was that one of the reasons for his coldness toward me? My uncle had known a great love once and generosity: I knew that with every shovelful of earth that went into my aunt's grave. He couldn't tell me or anybody else he hadn't had *that* opportunity. But I knew this also: *my father loved me, and my uncle had never really forgiven me for that.*

I remember the scene of the kiss came back to me once years later, long after my uncle had remarried, when he cautioned me, now alone in the world, unmarried and with both my parents dead, against possibly getting too intimate with my many friends, both in this country and abroad: friends could let you down, he said. (Did he imply that your family never would?) I remembered it again and again when I saw him seeming to lavish on his stepchildren and their children the affection he had never shown me. (Had he changed or was it something else?) Finally, I remembered it when I got word of his death—once when I was out of the country—and learned that his second wife, who was also "undemonstrative," had had his funeral not in the Methodist church, where he had been a steward for fifty years, but in the local funeral home; and she had buried him not beside his first wife, as I learned he had apparently intended, but in her own family's lot, beside her own parents. And they were not any of them people I could imagine ever dancing a jig on the front porch or anywhere else. One of the cousins wrote me the details, and she said she was glad I hadn't been there.

He didn't remember me in his will either, but I hadn't expected him to. My mother had told me years ago, not long after he had married again, that that would be the case. And as in most judgements concerning individual people and human nature in general, she had been right. But there were many memories left and especially that memory of the kiss that I could never forget. (Was that a kind of legacy?) Had I tried to read too much into it and thus deceived myself about a lot of things then? I've wondered about it ever since, maybe wondered even more as the years have gone on and I've seen more of life. And I still don't know. But I didn't make it up; it really did happen, just like I've said. And I did see it. And nobody can ever take it away from me now.

"The Lake!" It was a phrase that meant anything and everything when I was growing up. Long Lake, right down under the bluff, on the way to the River (there was only one river of course for us—the Mississippi); and it was second only to Reelfoot in size—that is, for "natural" lakes—nothing of the man-made TVA lakes about *it*. (Reelfoot of course was "natural" with a vengeance—formed by the cataclysmic earthquakes of 1811–1812, when the River ran backwards for twenty minutes and filled in the vast declivities generated thereby.) And people from Woodville—usually the hunting and drinking crowd—had houses down there, where God knows what went on. Or that's what some people thought. In the old days, when people really went camping down there, before any of the houses were built, they stayed in tents—one for the men, another for the women, and one for the cook and kitchen. And I've heard my mother say they had high old times down there back then.

But that was before the houses were built, which may have seemed— or people thought they did—an occasion for and incitement to sin. And card-playing—with " spot" cards, which was to say the kind you played bridge and poker with—was in evidence and even of course a whiskey bottle or two. Some of the older crowd, who probably had reservations about such high-stepping diversions, played forty-two, which was more or less like dominos played with cards, only the colors were reversed, with the dots being black on a white background. And it was apparently unique to Woodville. Indeed, I never knew of its being played anywhere else except Texas, which I learned when I lived out there many years ago. But then, as my mother said, you could gamble with *any* game, spot cards or no: that attitude seemed irrelevant if not downright silly to her, uncompromising realist that she always was. But every summer one of the "lake crowd," who was a judge on the appellate bench in Nashville, came down and staged a forty-two tournament at his house, which was more or less the highlight of the summer season for the older folks. So they could have their fun too and yet still be respectable.

The menu for all these festivities was of course catfish or crappie or whatever else was going at the time in the lake—and of course all fried in corn meal and grease, which I never cared for. (I never liked water-melon either—it was too watery and too sweet; so I always somehow felt disloyal to the South, though I could hold my own with anybody when it came to turnip greens.) But never mind, it was all part of the outdoors thing—hunting and fishing and all the rest; and the fleas went with the dog. And there were all sorts of tales told about the things that went on down there (and the lake was always "down," in itself a word of some sinister connotations), especially after the houses came in and the tents went out. (Of course in the old days all the parties were heavily cha-peroned: tents seemed to call for that but somehow not the houses.) And tales got told and cats got let out of the bag aplenty.

One of the most memorable occurrences—or at least it was supposed to have happened—had to do with the night some of the bright younger set got to rolling high, what with liquor and glandular stimulation—the sap rising, you might say—and decided to try putting the short pants which belonged to one of the young sons of the hosts on a very attractive lady member of the group. (She had such a "generous" figure that there was even some sort of bet on about whether or not the attempt would be successful—but it was.) Anyhow when the host couple, some time later, got involved in a lurid divorce trial, feeling was so high that everybody in town—back in Woodville, which was " up" on the bluff and so not susceptible to all the temptations of "down" at the lake—more or less took sides. And when the case came to trial, with the leading lawyers of the town involved and all sorts of shenanigans getting revealed about the didoes of the younger set *en route*, all who had been present were scared to death that the account of the pants episode would come out. (I don't remember whether it ever did: I was too young and all my information came by hearsay; but anyway it was hardly needed, there was so much to point your finger at. Why, people even went to the trial and took their lunches so they wouldn't have to give up their seats when they went home for their midday meal!)

On the whole, however, the lake and its environs were a masculine affair, I think. And there were lots of tales about what went on when the old boys were down there by themselves, with no feminine influence to soften and gentrify the atmosphere. I know they told the tale that old Mr. Larrimore, one of Woodville's leading graybeards, who lived on a rather imposing estate out on the edge of town—and my father said there never was a Larrimore in the world who didn't like to hunt and fish and drink too—was entertaining some of his older cronies down at his lake house—and it was all a strictly stag affair. And just to lend a respectable tone to the evening he invited the three leading preachers of the town—the Methodist, the Baptist, and the Presbyterian—as special guests and, on the sly, spiked the punch heavily and dispensed it quite liberally to one and all. And the preachers all got "elevated" and began to tell tales, sometimes even lapsing into a hymn or two or even, what was worse, a rather seamy-sided vaudeville song, like "My Cutie is Due on the Two-Two-Two" or even "You Gotta See Mamma Every Night or You Can't See Mamma at All." And of course old Mr. Larrimore pretended to be scandalized at the "practical joke" one of the other guests must have played on the group. But I think most people suspected he was the villain of the piece himself, and some of them even remarked that it was a good thing Woodville didn't have either a Catholic or Episcopal church: *their* priests could have held their own any day in the week with Mr. Larrimore or anybody else there!

But the wildest tale that ever got told from down at the lake had to do with Montelle Hill, the local undertaker who was in business with his father-in-law, old Mr. Waterfield, in a furniture store down on the Square, with the furniture side of things going on on the ground floor and the undertaking enterprise going on upstairs.

Montelle had always been something of a rounder or, as some people would say, a ring-tail tooter or even a ring-tail tooter with a glass eye; and he had a pretty raw sense of humor too. But apparently that sort of thing went with the funeral business. And when you got to dealing with dead folks and all such, it looked like there were no holds barred. (Their conventions were supposed to be a riot.) And they even told it on Montelle that he wasn't above fixing up a corpse with a salacious leer on his face, especially somebody who had spent his life as a deacon in the Baptist church, and then telling the family he had tried his best but he just couldn't get the sweet and peaceful smile on the man's face he was usually able to because he was too far gone with rigor mortis! For the 1940 election he was even supposed to have fastened a "Win with Wilkie" button on the broad and ample bosom of one of his "clients," a very proper matron who was a lifelong Democrat. And of course some really lewd souls even said they would be afraid to have Montelle "fix" *any* of their female relatives, there was no telling what he might do.

Whatever the case, Montelle was generally liked among the old boys in Woodville. I always had a sneaking idea they envied his situation: after all, nobody was going to argue much with an undertaker about his work, and nobody wanted to be there when he did it, and so you might say he had a free hand with life and death and a good deal else. But he had his crosses too because he had married into one of the oldest and most prominent families in the town—as they would have been the first to tell you. A lot of folks thought he had done it for old Mr. Waterfield's money, to get the capital to buy into the business with. In any case, he had married the oldest of the Waterfield daughters, who had decided in her younger days that her mission in life was to enjoy poor health and being waited on, and she was the apple of her old father's eye. And she spent her days—and nights too—making Montelle step around right lively. I don't know what she was like in the conjugal relationship, as they say; most people would have found it difficult to imagine her in the role. But whatever favors she had I should think she dispensed rarely and only subject to good behavior on the part of her husband. *Naturally* (or that's what people said) she had had a hysterectomy shortly after they were married and was even said to have run screaming out of the doctor's office in Memphis when he told her if she would just think less about her organs and more about her husband, both she and her love life would improve. And I think she just lived on laxatives, whether medicinal or natural, plus an enema from time to time just for instance.

Most people really felt kind of sorry for Montelle despite his reputation: whatever he did or didn't do, in the line of work or even pleasure. (One time after he first came to Woodville, the officers even caught him with a black woman having "relations" in a discarded packing case out in the alley behind the Woodville Dry Goods Company and just nailed them up therein and proceeded to roll them down the hill into one of the ravines Woodville was known for: *that* would teach him.) But most people thought it was more of a joke than anything else.

Whatever the case, after he married, as well as his wife, who was named Una Jean, he had all her family to contend with. Early in their marriage they had even lived with her parents, so there wasn't much Montelle did—or thought about doing—that went unobserved by the old man, whom Una Jean always called "Father," which I always thought must have made him seem like an Old Testament patriarch rather than somebody's daddy. But finally Montelle and Una Jean were able to move out into a house of their own (undertaking was always a lucrative business, I had been told); so at least Montelle was now spared that much. Everybody in town was really more or less on his side by that time too, even the ladies. But then ladies perhaps are always more realistic about such things than men, and of course Montelle always was a charmer.

But what really turned the tide of public opinion in his favor, you might say, was something that happened not long after they moved into their new house. And I suppose Montelle was not backward now about asserting his independence. He was making enough money and didn't have to live with his in-laws any longer, and Una Jean didn't hold the whip hand over him as much as she used to—or would still like to, most folks thought. And he *was* an attractive man. So a lot of his buddies and even the general public were inclined to overlook his peccadilloes with, "O, leave him alone: he's married to the meanest woman in the world!" Now whether he was tomcatting around a good deal on the side or not I don't know, but again "women" were always thought to be available at some of the stag affairs down at the lake: that was obviously a natural "venue." And there was a notorious "hotel" right down the road from the camp ground run by a man whom my father called a regular *outlaw* named Pegleg Jenkins on account of him being run over in the early days of automobiles by a Model T Ford the first time he ever saw one and it scared him.

Anyhow, the word got out that one night just before Christmas, when everybody was feeling a bit festive, some of the old boys had a party down at one of their houses at the lake. And there was a good deal of drinking of course, even, it was said, some crap-shooting. Of course there were a good many salty jokes recounted and naturally a lot of tale-telling about their sexual exploits past and present, including a good deal of boasting about what might have been called their vital statistics, mostly concerned with the "equipment" with which the respective men had been endowed by their Creator. That was a sure indicator, they all thought, of how much they could "do," how much they could "handle." Of course the only way they could settle it was by outright exhibition, about which of course none of them was bashful. But how to make such "measure-ments"? There didn't seem to be a ruler or even a yard stick on the premises, but all of a sudden somebody suggested there were enough *sil-ver dollars* between them all (and of course this dates my story) to make use of them as some sort of homemade measuring device. So that's what they did, each of them in turn displaying his "organ" on the table top and lining up beside it enough silver dollars to get the job done. But it was soon evident that there really wasn't going to be any sort of contest: like Abou Ben Adhem, Montelle's name led all the rest. And when the rest of the old sports saw what he had to offer (seven silver dollars' worth), they drew back almost as if a wild elephant had been let loose in their midst, giggling, snorting, even spouting some very choice profanity spoken more in wonderment than in vexation. But the consensus seemed to be, as one of the bolder spirits among them put it, "Lord God, I never expected to say so, but for the first time in my life, I really feel sorry for Una Jean!"

What Have They Done?

In my hometown there was a family of three sisters and three brothers whose surname was Larrimore, and they always gave you to understand that they had lived there longer than anybody else and maybe even founded the place—or their ancestors had. Anyhow, they acted like they had all been there since before Christ, my mother said. They lived out on the edge of town in a big white house called Larrimore Lodge; and when I was a little boy and went out there to see them, along with my parents, I was tremendously impressed because they had peacocks, some all colors, some all white, parading all over the front lawn, in and out of the boxwood shrubs. And I was both fascinated and terrified by them: it was my first encounter with the exotic outside the confines of the picture show or the zoo. Later on, I remember crying bitterly because one of the Larrimore sisters was getting married—out on the front lawn—and everybody in the county was going to be there. But I had to be left at home because Miss Lina (she was the one getting married) had decreed that there were to be *no children* present. And I had always like weddings and graduations, even funerals: children love any kind of ceremony, you know. And they are born dramatists.

Anyhow, it wasn't long until I was reading *Gone with the Wind* and books about the Civil War and Southern history. And I decided that Larrimore Lodge was right out of the white-columned grandeur I had been reading about and the Larrimores themselves probably were all as romantic and Technicolorful as all get-out. Because for one thing, although they were all still fairly young, their parents were dead and they all lived out there at Larrimore Lodge by themselves and kept the family going, which I thought very brave and dashing of them. (Almost like Scarlett and all the others at Tara during Reconstruction.) Furthermore, I understood that, in their will, their parents had specified that the house was to be lived in only by the unmarried children: the others, the ones who had gotten married (and until now none of them had), could visit there only for a month at the time and then only at the invitation of the rest. And it was all *entailed* too. Everybody thought it a funny kind of will, maybe even an irreverent one. Why, my father said, they were all acting like Larrimore Lodge was some sort of *shrine*. And he supposed they would have entailed it all *in perpetuity* if they could have; but, thank God, this was *America*. But my mother said what difference did it make because of course there was nobody in the world good enough for the Larrimores anyhow (they thought); and they would probably rather just live out there by themselves and never marry and so end up just sitting there looking at each other anyway! And where would be the perpetuity in that?

She said she remembered one time some years ago when old Miss Bessie Maxwell, who lisped and *had* lived in town since before Christ and said of the other old families that she'd seen them come and she'd seen them go but *she* was still there, got put out with how the Larrimore sisters always took themselves so seriously and expected other folks to do the same. ("Our family have always been leaders in the community," they would say. "And we were all brought up to carry on in the tradition.") And she bristled up one day, when she'd heard all that sort of thing once too often and turned to my mother and spewed out: "People alwayth thay, 'The Larrimore girlth are tho talented, the Larrimore girlth are tho talented,' but now, I athk you, jutht what have they done?" And I could tell that my mother felt something of the same way: she never was one who thought you could spend your life just sitting on the front porch looking pretty or poring over your family tree and living off your ancestors, which was just another form of *living on capital*, a mortal sin. You had to be up and doing and look sharp in this world: "sit stiddy, look nateral, wink reglar, and keep your eye on the *feudlam*," as an old-time photographer had told her aunt Fannie years ago. One way or another, you had to earn your board and keep here, my mother thought; and it wouldn't be with your ancestors or your looks. Looks had never gotten her anywhere, she said; and as for ancestors, that was nothing to *your* credit. The real question was whether *you* could be worthy of *them*. And she thanked God every day you could choose your friends.

But anyhow, when I was growing up, the Larrimores and Larrimore Lodge became some sort of symbol for me—of the past and the Old South and high romance, I suppose, all suffused with some sort of remote glamour. My grandfather (my father's father), who was a Virginian, had fought in the Civil War and had been at Appomattox Courthouse too; and he was still alive. But I didn't think he was particularly romantic or glamorous because he was deaf and chewed tobacco and the juice ran down and stained his beard and he didn't like to bathe either. And there wasn't anything remote about him. He was cranky as the devil too, and I was afraid of him because he was so old. And that may have been something of the way my mother felt about the Larrimores. "Why, the Larrimores think they're all just *broken out* with aristocracy; and that old house of theirs—which I wouldn't have if you gave it to me—just the next thing to Mount Vernon," she said. "And it was nothing in this world but logs covered over with weather-boarding until the last years of their parents' lives when somebody had the bright idea of making it look like an 'old colonial home.' So they brought this big highfalutin architect out from Memphis—named *Denaux*, all very French, and I can hear old Mrs. Larrimore saying it right now, like it was honey to her mouth—to remodel the house and lay out a 'formal garden.' *That's* where all the boxwoods came from."

So I could tell that opinions differed not only about the Larrimores but also about their own opinion of themselves. Our Sunday School class, which was taught by Miss Lina Larrimore, the youngest one, was taken out there from time to time (for Easter egg hunts mostly, because of the big lawn) and then shown over the house and grounds. (Maybe that was why she didn't want any children at her wedding: she'd seen what they could be like when they were turned loose.) The high point always came when they took you into one of the parlors (the one on the right as you went in) which they had fixed up like a museum, with family portraits overlooking it all. And it was all devoted to history. They had their grandfather's Civil War uniform there and his sword (he had fought under General Nathan Bedford Forrest, they said) and some old cannon balls they'd found years ago on their farm down on the Mississippi near Fort Pillow. And one of the brothers had fought in World War I, so they had a spiked German helmet he had brought back from the battlefield. And I used to wonder what had happened to the soldier who had worn the helmet (of course if he was dead, he didn't need it anymore) and whether the Germans, who everybody said really were Huns and barbarians, had used those spikes in all their "atrocities" like bayoneting babies and cutting off the Belgian women's breasts. There was a spinning wheel too and some patchwork quilts, which the Larrimores said went back to pioneer days; but somehow they always implied that that part of the past was as well left quiet: they'd all come away from *that*. (My mother said they just didn't want you to mistake them for the coonskin-cap, hog-and-hominy crowd. Sometimes you could go *too far back*, even for the Larrimores.) And it was usually when you were in the parlor-museum that Miss Virginia, the oldest one of the sisters, told you how their grandmother had saved the silver from the Yankees: she buried it out in the family graveyard and made it all up to look like a new grave, complete with tombstone, which I for one thought damned clever of her.

The Larrimores were very hospitable people, and you could always go out to see them and take your friends from out of town because it *was* a sort of showplace. And the Larrimores would always perform too and tell all the old family tales like about when their great-uncle John Estes (where most of their land had come from) went through the Johns Hopkins clinic up in Baltimore along with his old friend, Colonel Hendrix, who had been in Congress; and when they asked him for his financial statement when he checked in, he said he didn't do anything but make a cotton crop and cut timber when he could but Colonel Hendrix told them he himself was a "landowner and planter." So Great-uncle John got charged only the minimum fee, but Colonel Hendrix got *soaked*; and of course Great-uncle John could have *bought and sold* him any day in the week, they all laughed. And then there was the time way back yonder when Cousin Monroe Larrimore was shot down and killed in cold blood right on the Square by the sheriff, and his wife was left a widow with small children and feeling was so high she even had to leave the state and go *up North* to live for a while. Why, the sheriff might have been *lynched*, the Larrimores said, and the families had never spoken since.

But my father said everybody knew "Cousin Monroe" had been drunk as a lord and he was mean into the bargain, though it had all been over and done with lo, these many years. And he had *made* the sheriff kill him, really: he drew on him first. "But that's what you get into when you get to delving back into the past," my father said. "You may find something you hadn't counted on. That's just like the Larrimores to want to dress it all up and make it sound nice and sweet, with a 'feud' and all other sorts of historical foolishness thrown in for good measure. But the plain truth is otherwise, and somebody ought to rise up sometime and tell them so."

But anyhow, the Larrimores and Larrimore Lodge were always there, no matter where I went or what I did—off to school, off to work, travel in foreign parts, the whole business. And in many ways, they never seemed to change. Miss Lina, my Sunday School teacher, did get married to a doctor from Nashville—on the lawn, as I said. And the oldest son, Madison, the one who had brought the German helmet back, finally married a girl from Memphis and went to live down there. But both of them still spent as much time as possible at Larrimore Lodge, and both of them still referred to it as home. I used to wonder what their husbands and wives, to say nothing of *their* families, would think of all that *clannishness*, which was a word people always used when they spoke of the Larrimores. I know it did get out that Miss Lina's husband, the doctor, was home with her one time and the Larrimores were all going to convene—all six of them—to discuss some of the family financial affairs, their "holdings," as they always called them. And he expected of course to take part in the discussion too. But the Larrimores just politely asked him to wait outside: this was *family* business! And he thought it was all more funny than anything else and told somebody, and that was how people knew.

The rest of the Larrimores stayed home. Jamieson, who was next after Madison in age, managed their "holdings," which were mostly a lot of land in the Mississippi Bottom. Estes had something of a law practice in town; but his heart was mostly down in the Bottom too, where he loved to go hunting and fishing, as often as he could manage. ("That's the Larrimore in him," said my father, "and maybe the lawyer too. I never knew a Larrimore yet that didn't pride himself, rightly or wrongly, on being something of a sport. And lawyers just have a natural affinity for that way of life. Lawyers and hunters and fishermen—they're all *born liars*!") The other two sisters, Miss Virginia and Miss Susan, stayed home too. Miss Virginia kept the house and said she had tried to succeed her mother as "hostess," and Miss Susan taught the first grade. And neither of them showed any sign of getting married. As far as anybody knew, they were perfectly content with their lot, living out there at Larrimore Lodge, on the edge of town but not *of* the town, and entertaining their friends with tales of the Larrimore history and all the rest.

It all used to worry me, though, after I got older, especially after I had gone off to school up north. What would my friends up there make of them? Would they just think it all silly, maybe all rather sad—to have nothing in your life but that old house and all that history? Weren't the Larrimores just playing right into the hands of all those people up north or anywhere else who wanted to see the South and Southerners in nothing but stereotyped roles? Wouldn't the best thing that could happen to them be for them suddenly all to be transported hundreds of miles away, where nobody had ever heard of either them or Larrimore Lodge or their damned history? (After all, it was no news to any of *us*: history was just something you *had*.) Maybe I had just had enough of the Southern thing for awhile, but I was really right tired of them now and the whole idea of them, to tell the truth. And I thought of Miss Bessie Maxwell and wondered really, *what had they done*. What indeed?

After I graduated from college, I went to work in Chicago and traveled around the country a good bit and even got sent to Europe a couple of times on business. So I didn't see the Larrimores any more for several years. But the first time I came back for Christmas, I found an invitation from them asking me to an "Old-Fashioned Christmas Day Open House." And I reckoned they would all be dolled up in hoop skirts and knee breeches if not powdered wigs if they thought they could get away with it. But I thought I'd like to go out anyway to see them in action one more time; it would probably be amusing, and they weren't going to live forever. So I did, and all the younger set were there, as well as the old reliables. (The Larrimores always liked young people, I remembered. Yeah, I thought, that way they would always have a new audience to perform for.) But anyhow, there was lots of eggnog (out of Grandma's cut glass punch bowl), and it wasn't weak stuff either. And there were also country ham and beaten biscuits and fruit cake that had been aged in brandy—the whole Yuletide shebang. And naturally, holly and mistletoe everywhere.

Miss Lina and her husband (big-city doctor reduced temporarily to prince-consort status, I supposed) were there from Nashville and Madison and his wife from Memphis. (He bought cotton down on Front Street, but they came home to Larrimore Lodge nearly every weekend.) Miss Virginia was being gracious all over the place—gray now and getting more stately all the time: she would be achieving Dowager Duchess status before long, I thought. And Miss Susan was showing everybody around as though they were all first-graders. But there were no grandchildren, and somehow I didn't think there ever would be. Jamieson and Estes, looking like "distinguished older men" with graying temples, were circulating around with the eggnog, as courtly as ever. There were faithful black retainers in and out of both the dining room and the kitchen and of course out front parking the cars. And the scene was complete, just as advertised: "the mixture as before" and apparently just where I had come in, when as a child I had first gone out there to see the peacocks. And I wouldn't have missed it for the world.

That was all a good while ago—back in the early sixties, before the troubles of either civil rights or Vietnam became acute; so the wider world didn't impinge much on the conversation, which, after the exchange of season's greetings, was mostly about that fall's crops and plans for the new high school. But not long before I left I did hear somebody ask Miss Virginia what she thought about our town's having a "pilgrimage" in the spring and opening the old houses to visitors for a week or so, all in aid of various local good works, something on the order of what they did in Natchez and Holly Springs though of course we couldn't possibly compete with them in numbers or in splendor. Larrimore Lodge would be a "natural" for such an undertaking, it was urged. But Miss Virginia demurred. "The very idea!" she protested. "We love having our friends come out to see us, but we're not on display for the entertainment of perfect strangers. And we've always prided ourselves on the hospitality of Larrimore Lodge. It would be simply unthinkable to charge admission for that, no matter how worthy the cause. After all, this is our *home!*" And then she went on to tell somebody else about Grandma hiding the silver from the Yankees in the graveyard.

Yes, it was all perfect—just like a movie set or Colonial Williamsburg, I reflected as I drove back to my parents' house. But no, it wasn't just flies in amber either. I didn't think the Larrimores were acting it all out: their roles now really were indistinguishable from their lives and their house really was a home. And if they were acting, it was perhaps not so much for us as for themselves. You might be amused by them, even sometimes a little unhappy for them. But you finally had to hand it to them. They were living out their dream, and it was all coming true. Or at any rate, all coming true for them.

POSTSCRIPT. Well, it's nearly thirty years later now; and I suppose you're wondering how it all came out and what happened to the Larrimores and Larrimore Lodge in due course. The Larrimores themselves are all gone now: none of that generation was particularly long-lived. And no, there never were any grandchildren to inherit under the entail. But the last survivor—ironically, Miss Virginia, who had been the oldest of them all —was able to arrange for Larrimore Lodge, its contents and grounds, all to become the property of the county historical society after all the farm land had reverted to some distant cousins. (I remembered what she had said at that Christmas Day open house: she had evidently changed her mind since then.) And so now it stands there as "a memorial to more gracious days and ways and a gentle family that are gone." That's what it says on a stone marker right beside the front gate just before you head up the long drive bordered by the boxwoods. I don't know who wrote the inscription: it sounds a good deal like Miss Virginia herself. But I thought it all looked fine when I went out to see the place the last time I was back to visit—all pretty much just like it used to be except that I didn't see any peacocks. It's open to the public several days a week now, and the younger generation in particular are delighted with it: they say it would have been "neat" to live in a place like that and they wish they could have known the Larrimores. And I say yes indeed but tell them I still miss the peacocks.

Feeding the Stock

She was born to love somebody, and she had done it all her life. An only child, she had only her mother and father at home, out in the country. But of course there was the Methodist church right down the road, the center of the neighborhood. And then of course she started to school in town. The county superintendent wanted her to go to school out in the neighborhood where she lived; but her mother, who had been the highest paid secretary in Richmond, Virginia, before she married, was ambitious for her and insisted that she start school in town, the county seat, four miles away. So her father began taking her in every day in the old Model T (and in the surrey when the roads were too bad), alternating with another father down the road, who took her, along with his own two daughters, on alternate weeks. And so it went all the way through school.

Whether she ever thought of going off to college when she graduated from high school, I don't know: times were hard (back in the Depression) and she never forgot the sight of all that cotton standing in the fields because nobody would buy it and in consequence never voted anything but Democratic all her life long. But college wasn't that important to her right then because she had already found her vocation in music. Whether she had a natural longing to learn to play the piano I don't know; perhaps at first she was only lukewarm about it. But her mother soon took command and would often sit beside her at the piano when she practiced, a switch in her hand, to see that she neither fainted nor failed. And she soon had gone through nearly every piano teacher in town and even given a high school certificate recital when she graduated.

But what was she to do then? For a while she studied with a very accomplished teacher, both for piano and organ, in the neighboring county; and whether she determined then that her "calling" would be that of a music teacher, I don't know. But before long it became apparent what lay ahead of her—to her and her parents both, I think. And a couple of years after she was out of high school she began forming her first classes, first in a small town only a couple of miles away (there was no resident teacher there then), then later on transferring to the county seat where she had gone to school. And she prospered. She had a natural way with children, it seemed, and the younger the better, she said, beginning no later than the first grade. And she began to do all the things expected of piano teachers then—forming a music club, where her pupils had their first taste of playing before a real audience and where also they learned something of music history and the conduct of organizational affairs—

parliamentary law and such like, in short their first halting steps toward learning the life of the group, perhaps the life of society itself. She entered her pupils in all the regional competitions too, not only because it was a means of showing her handiwork but also because they would thereby broaden their horizons both at home and in the wider reaches of the county and the state itself. And her reputation grew accordingly: soon there would be more than one generation who had "taken" from "Miss Laura," as she came increasingly to be known.

But all the time people wondered whether that was all her life was to be. Certainly it had already proved itself to be a life of service—playing for church, playing for weddings (never refusing a funeral if she could possibly help it), building her life around her parents, her teaching, her community, all the immemorial activities of a professional spinster. But what about marriage, children, a home, and all else expected of any woman in those days? Was she unhappy and frustrated about that? Nobody ever knew: she just kept on with her teaching and all her other duties, perhaps thinking the Lord would provide in His own good time if it was His will. And as far as anybody knew, she was a happy woman and one whose life seemed fulfilled in all she did.

The years went along of course and suddenly a man did indeed appear on the scene, from over in the next county but with family ties in her own too and a background very similar—Presbyterian rather than Methodist but farming, the country, rural pursuits, especially hunting, even singing tenor in his church choir. And everybody wondered how it could all have worked out better. And they all—her students past and present, the community and county themselves—were happy for her. After all, her parents weren't going to live forever, and somehow it wasn't *right* for her to live all her life out there in the country with no exposure to a larger world. So it was all a happy event when the marriage took place, and she went to live with her husband on his farm twenty miles away. But that was all soon to change because her father died very suddenly only a year later, and the newly married couple moved back to her old home, to be with her mother and of course, for her husband, to look after the farm. (Apparently, they had made a bargain: he said he would manage her father's place but he didn't want to leave his church. So this lifelong Methodist duly left the church where she had played for services nearly every Sunday of her life, and became a Presbyterian and in due course organist for her new affiliation.)

And then a year later there was a baby, a little boy named for her father; and again everybody was delighted because she was now definitely in the fulfilled state of married life and safe from spinsterhood and solitude. She kept right on teaching too, with her mother more or less bringing up the son—and gladly too because she said she would have been miserable after her husband died, with nothing now to do. And of course the grandson duly came to adore her. It really did seem that everything had turned out right for all of them too: a continuingly useful life, both professionally and socially, a fruitful marriage and a real future to look forward to in generations yet to come. And behind it all love and affection for the family and all else among the traditional values. And "Miss Laura" never stopped; in fact she took on more pupils than she had ever had before. And then when her mother in her last years became an invalid, she took over the management of her illness, and all the household chores as well. Of course she had faithful old Bessie, who had lived right there on the farm all those years (and was the daughter of old Aunt Sally who had been born into slavery). And down the road was old Uncle Bud who had lived on the place almost as long, a handyman and jack of all trades. And she could delegate much to them both. Of course there was her husband too, now dividing his time between their place and his own. But behind it all she herself stood, overseeing, supervising, not a *boss* but a *giver*, a *lover* even, not from any self-conscious devotion to duty but simply because it was in her nature. And she did it unthinkingly: whoever had to *think* about love? You didn't do that any more than you thought about music or any of the other "finer things," as she called them. And yes, she taught all day long too, but supper was on the table every night at six o'clock.

In due course her mother died, and the son married and moved away. Her husband's health wasn't any too good now either, and they finally decided to rent out the farm. But she kept right on teaching, well into her sixties, then later her seventies. And to all questions about retirement, she would simply smile and say she intended to keep right on teaching as long as old Dr. Houston, who had a little farm right down the road and was even older than she was, approved. And besides, what would she do with herself then? I don't suppose anybody in her life had ever seen her just sit down in a rocking chair and fold her hands. One time she did say if she simply had to give up teaching music, she would still like to work with children in some way, perhaps helping them learn to read. But anybody that knew her at all would know she wasn't thinking about going into a retirement home or any such. Who on earth wanted to sit up there all day long and hear old folks talk about their ailments and their grandchildren? And she hoped the Lord would deliver her from that.

But of course the clock kept right on ticking. She herself stayed well and just as busy as ever, but her husband began to fail, with heart disease and some other ailments. And for some months he was in and out of the hospital, with more than one specialist overseeing his case. But again "Miss Laura" went right on teaching, commuting back and forth to the hospital in Memphis every few days but still working, still involved, in the full context of her life. And finally not long before Christmas they were able to bring her husband home. But anybody that looked at him would almost have known he was nearing the end, over eighty now too. And that was what finally happened, a few days after Christmas, which they had spent with the son and his family, who lived about fifty miles away.

She woke very early that morning, shortly before daybreak and heard him get up to go to the bathroom, then returning to his own bed, falling across her own. And she knew this time it was something very serious. But calmly as ever she called Dr. Houston and when his wife answered asked whether he was up. And of course he was, said his wife, out feeding the stock as usual. So Laura asked whether he could come right up when he got them all fed, she was afraid her husband was having a heart attack and a very serious one. But naturally he came on right that minute: for the moment the stock would have to wait. But by the time he got there it was no longer any use. Miss Laura's husband was gone.

Of course he stayed right there with her till he had called all the neighbors and kinfolks and notified the undertaker and didn't leave until after the body had been removed. He told somebody later he had no thought of leaving "Miss Laura" alone at a time like that, even as strong a character as he knew her to be. But as soon as the house filled up with people, she went over to him and put her arms around him and said, "You've done all you can do now. So go on back home and finish feeding the stock. That's where you belong now." "But what about you, what will you do now?" he wanted to know. "O, don't worry about me," she said, "because the first of next week I'm going to start back to teaching. This part of my life is over now, and it's time for me to go on to the next one. And that of course means teaching. I've never really belonged anywhere else."

Brutally Massacred by Indians

"The earliest settlers on this site were brutally massacred by Indians," intoned the young woman who was reeling off her spiel in showing us around one of Virginia's stateliest houses down on the James. And of course my friend and I began to giggle. Part of the laughter, of course, came from the disparity between the guide's matter-of-factness (as though she were reading labels on the pantry shelf) and the horrors she was relating. Part also, of course, came from some apprehension of the house's original glory and subsequent decline, its current prosperity—all seen against the standard rags-to-riches saga so often depicted in American history, whether of people or places or things.

Because this stately house was alive and well and, you might say, thoroughly in business. Postcards were on sale, of course, but so also were dolls dressed as colonists, boxwood seedlings grown right there on the place, even preserves made by colonial "receipts." There was a tea room next door to the shop, both of them carefully created or recreated in the period—the shop remodeled from the original "bachelor's quarters," we were told, and the tea room a "reconstruction" carefully "researched" by specialists at The University. The young women guides of course were dressed in the period too—chintz skirts, mob caps, the whole lot.

And they had all done their homework: this was no mere souped-up spectacle of cash-and-carry history. There was a film about the house's beginnings, its building, early days, shown down in the cellar, as the first part of the tour; then guides took the various tour groups, in small numbers, up into the house itself. Everybody knew—or was supposed to know—what he was looking at.

The house's owners were old friends of mine; but it had been some time—several years, in fact—since I had last seen either them or the house. I knew that they were getting along in years; I had even heard that they both had been unwell, with the usual debilitating ailments that come to most of us if we live long enough—failing vision, unsteady legs, and all the rest. Indeed, I well remembered the first time I had been out to see them, the first time I had ever seen either them or the house; and the husband of the couple had pointed out to me the gazebo which had just been built on the front lawn, overlooking the James of course—the house's entrance when everything arrived and departed by the river. The summer house was a charming reconstruction—eighteenth-century chinoiserie, I assumed. But unlike many such reconstructions, this one came equipped with screens and an extension telephone, which my host explained as preparation for a future when he might be too old to go in after his own ice; he could then just give the kitchen a ring, and out would come reinforcements from the house.

I thought right then that he was a man to be reckoned with. And indeed, I had inferred as much from the common friends in Richmond who had introduced us. It was he, they told me, who had first gone up and down the James telling his neighbors in the other stately homes that they were all sitting on top of a gold mine and didn't know it! I suspect that, at first, they wrote him off as nothing more than the Yankee he was; and of course Colonial Williamsburg hadn't gotten good and started then. But times were hard: the Depression was still abroad in the land. And before long not only he but his neighbors were opening their houses to the public.

His name was Duncan McMath, and he had come down to Virginia as a young man, to help his father with the old broken-down estate he had bought, mostly for its timber. The old house, long unlived in, had more or less been thrown in with the deal. But it took Duncan's fancy from the start: indeed, he even began camping out in it, refusing to live in the bachelor's quarters, when he began acting as his father's overseer. When I got to know him, he even told me he had cooked over the open fire in one of the upstairs bedrooms, living in that one room with nothing much more in the way of furniture than a cot and rocking chair and, of course, only a lamp for light. There was none of the original furniture left, of course; and the principal rooms downstairs were more or less a shambles, the result of years of neglect and even downright abuse by successive farm tenants. Because that was what its former glory had sunk to—an old house that just went along with the place, no notice taken of its historic past or even its structural beauty. The Georgian outlines had even been defaced with Victorian porches, themselves now in disrepair.

But even then that house was becoming the great passion in his life. Did he, like so many "outsiders," fall a prey to the genius of the place, all the history that, you might say, was right there lying around loose? Surely, it was more than just the house's recollected beauty that began to obsess him. Did it take on symbolic meaning for him, something he wanted to restore and recover for his own life—someone who had probably up until then thought history was something that should be left safely to professionals if not altogether ignored? Whatever the case, he had always been more enthusiastic about it all, I was given to understand,

than his wife, who had been a local girl, Anne Harrison from Williamsburg. For her, I think, history was just something you had: there was no
need to make a production out of it. And I gather there were times when
she thought that was just the trouble with that part of the world, and
especially the part of it bounded by the James River: there was more
history on hand than could safely be consumed on the premises. And she
could take it or leave it. (But she had her history too—a descendant of
the Balls.) In some ways, that big house was something she'd been trying
to get away from all her life. She could go along with it, yes; she
wouldn't make trouble. But she didn't particularly relish the life she lived
on the house's second floor (the first was where the tourists passed
through), never knowing when some of the paying customers might erupt
upstairs, just to be sure they got their money's worth, even though there
were a couple of signs warning them that it was off-limits.

Some of all this I gleaned from the friends who had originally
introduced us; the rest they told me themselves, more or less. They told
me also—but Duncan mainly—how carefully they had worked to restore
the house to its former glory, doing a little this year, perhaps more the
next as the gate receipts allowed them to. There was none of the original
furniture left of course, but they had hunted compatible pieces all over
the country and once Duncan had even gone to England in search of
more. Their portraits in oils hung in the dining room too, painted years
ago when they were first married; but already they looked distinguished
and worthy of their surroundings—not just because of their elegant attire
either. It was as though both of them looked out at you, coolly and
serenely, to assure you that they knew where they were and what they
were doing and weren't presuming on anything, really. And in time they
and the house would be worthy of one another; in time they and the
house would be one.

And I found them a charming couple, whom I enjoyed knowing more
and more as the years went along. Anne was an amusing talker, and there
was little that went on up and down the river that she couldn't tell you
about. Duncan's interests were more restricted, mainly concentrated on
the house. And he made no bones about his feeling for it, even his
determination to make it pay for itself. ("When the Duke of Bedford—
you know, the one who owns Woburn Abbey—was visiting down at
Williamsburg last year, they brought him out to see us and of course the
house: they all said it would be Greek meeting Greek! And it was too!")
And then again: "I've got over six hundred acres here, with some cattle

and corn and some pasture, but my best crop of course is the tourists!"
And Anne would say, the Lord knew that was so and she might as well
be married to a lawn-mower, Duncan got up so early to get going in the
summer. The house was open every day in the year but Christmas Day,
too.

The McMaths had a son and daughter, but they lived in Richmond—
not very much interested in the house, I gathered. (Had they had too
much history from kindergarten on up?) And I sometimes idly wondered
what they would do with the house when they entered into possession. I
was sure Duncan would want them to carry right on when he was gone,
but of course they might have other ideas, even if it was all a money-
making proposition. It wasn't everybody in the world who would want
to build his life around a house; and I thought of Thoreau, who was
flooded with relief when the man who had made a trade with him to sell
his farm backed out because his wife changed her mind.

That house had held Duncan down nearly all his life, but then perhaps he didn't want to go anywhere either. In any case, it was his life and
his passion. What did it prove? I wasn't sure. But I could tell that it was
living history to him, not just the museum kind. ("Look, we're living
right here where all those old folks lived, and the house is a working
house and the farm is a working farm. It's not just a sideshow. And that's
the way it's going to stay. Maybe it's like they say and we're *conserving*
it, not just *preserving* it. But the main thing is that it keeps on going. It's
life, not just a game we're playing.") What was it for Anne? Something
of prison, at best a dear enemy? No matter, I thought. The house was
Duncan's pride and joy, and she was Duncan's wife. Whatever the case,
I thought, Duncan and Anne were a remarkable couple, living in an extra-
ordinary house.

And as time passed and I got to know the McMaths better, saw them
pretty well handling whatever life sent them with no complaints, I kept
going back in my mind to that earlier time I had been to see them, when
the guide had said the earliest settlers on the place had been brutally
massacred by Indians. That sounded fine in the history books, though I
always wondered just how else you could carry out a massacre if not
brutally; and it sounded even better in a travelogue if you kept it all low-
keyed. But then so what else was new? The Indians were gone; but the
bus loads of tourists had arrived, even parties coming downriver from
Richmond by excursion steamer, and on one occasion the governor himself arriving for some function by helicopter on the front lawn. And you

had to watch every last one of them too, to make sure they didn't steal anything or what they didn't steal, deface. Duncan and Anne had told me often enough that they could write a book about it all. But you had to learn not to let it get you down. History was full of such things— massacres, ambushes, lynchings, you name it—a rotten business. And it was problematic what you ever learned from any of it—maybe just that nobody ever learned anything much but went right on fighting and killing and lying and stealing and all the rest.

And yet there was another side too. In some ways, you might survive a massacre if you knew what it was all about, understood what was involved in the business: the violence wasn't altogether random, and the bullets didn't just come ticketed "to whom it may concern." There was some sort of rhyme and reason to it. Had Duncan learned any of that? Surely, he wasn't just playing with history, playing at history, as I suspected they always were in Williamsburg. O, yes, he was turning a pretty penny out of the house; but I think he loved it too, the facts he kept digging up about it (the first place this had happened, the first place that was done, in the colonies and later under the new republic), all the restorations he continued to make. He was enormously proud of it all, what it was, what it proved. And I think in a way Anne was too. That was the way I felt more than ever, during my most recent visit there, just last week—finding them both somewhat the worse for age and wear and yet giving no sign of surrender. It was just like old times, too, with the talk as good as any I had ever heard there—and this despite the heat of the long summer twilight. The gazebo with its extension telephone was still right there on the front lawn overlooking the James, and that was where we sat and had our drinks.

Over the Mountains

Over the mountains we came, three of us who had been his friends, driving early on that Good Friday morning from East Tennessee down into the South Carolina Piedmont, to bury him and then ponder on the significance of his life and death. He had taken his own life—a shock to all of us. I myself had seen him only the week before and would never have thought such a thing was on his mind. Indeed, he had seemed very much concerned when I told him about my own recent loss—the death of the last of my aunts; and then he had gone on to tell a common friend that he was worried about me, I seemed so depressed. But no, I should never have thought of him as suicidal, which of course just goes to prove you never know anything about anybody. In some ways, we're always strangers to each other.

He had had sorrow of course. He and his wife had been divorced—a great surprise in itself; I had thought them very happy. And she had ended up with the two daughters—teenagers and already quite pretty— and gone back to teaching school. He himself had gone on to finish his graduate degree in history, then become director of the local library's historical collection—the perfect man for the job, I thought, because of his own enthusiasm for the subject and his great flair for meeting the public and of course for raising money. It was all now a great loss to the community.

And now as we drove on, I had a lot to think about. Jim and I had been friends for some years though I wasn't a real intimate of his. He was great fun of course, a fine *raconteur* naturally, and unfailingly warm and outgoing. Many people would have thought he had the very joy of life in him, blood and bone—everything to live for, as we say. But no, there had been something dark inside, something perhaps eating on him that I had never suspected. Oh, we used to kid each other about our respective forebears and origins. I was a West Tennessean—a native of the most "Southern" part of the state, really an extension of northern Mississippi; and my grandfather had been a Confederate soldier, a private in the Army of Northern Virginia who had been at Appomattox. But I had often teased Jim about being only a mountaineer at heart, for all his own vaunted Southern past: some ancestor somewhere along the line had voted for the South Carolina secession ordinance in 1860, I think. But he always said I was a Southerner only by courtesy: my grandfather had left the Old Dominion after the War to settle in the tall and uncut of West Tennessee. And anyway Tennessee had been the last state to secede but

South Carolina had been the first, to which I had retorted, yes, but he wasn't a Charlestonian by any means. But, like all Southerners, we had told each other enough about our families and their eccentricities and peculiarities to furnish substance, ammunition for a good deal of fun. And yes, that was the word: fun—no booger bears there for either of us. He and Carol had been fun to be around, whether as hosts or as guests. And he could charm birds out of the trees with the stories about his relatives.

And I recall two such instances now. One was the tale about the time Cousin Sophronia Scott arrived an hour late for a bridal luncheon in honor of her daughter at the Atlanta Biltmore and apologized to the hostess for her tardiness in a stage whisper, audible to one and all, to the effect that when she had gotten up that morning, she had found that her bowels were just *locked* and she had had to take *two* enemas. And there was always the story about plain-spoken Great-aunt Ida Pickens, whom someone got by mistake on the telephone one time under the impression that she was the Mrs. Pickens whose husband had a small machine shop in his backyard and asked whether he was still sharpening lawn mowers, to which Great-aunt Ida had replied that he had been dead for five years and she didn't know what he was doing now. These were two of the best—vintage, you might say, and pure Jim. (He always maintained that Southern women were the ultimate realists.)

But now I was to see his parents and other family, indeed his home-town, for the first time. What an irony, I thought, to get my first glimpse of the characters, the places he had made come alive only now, in the context of his death. And yes, it was *Good* Friday too, which name used to disturb me in my Methodist childhood because of course I couldn't see a thing *good* about it. There was a further complication: my own father had been buried on Good Friday, and he too had died a sudden though not a violent death—just collapsed with a heart attack at the breakfast table and died right there before our eyes. Another great shock but of course he was an old man. But no, there hadn't been anything *good* about any of it. It was just life.

But these musings were all peculiar to me. The two friends I was traveling with doubtless had their thoughts too. Harry, who was driving, had been Jim and Carol's neighbor for some years—an anesthesiologist, a "big rich doctor," whom Jim used to accuse of making his living by putting people to sleep, to which Harry always responded that well, un-like some others, he didn't make his way in the world by simply boring people to death about family trees and the dim dark past. (Jim was always full of tales about helping blue-haired dowagers with their genealogical research.) Linda, our companion, no longer lived in our part of the world: she had married a Yankee and now lived in Massachusetts. But she had been a close friend of Jim and Carol's and ironically had arrived for her annual visit "home" only the night before, just in time to get the news of Jim's death. So we were all three somewhat subdued now, thinking our own thoughts about Jim and the sadness which must have overcome him yet, as always happens, laughing when we thought of yet one more "Jim story," as we called the great flood of anecdote that seemed his natural element. Cheerfulness does keep breaking in at such times, along with an enormous appetite, I've noticed—prompted perhaps by the necessity of individuals to preserve and renew life in the presence of the Great Enemy. We all remembered different "sides" of Jim, but they all coalesced now to establish a composite likeness to which we gave assent. Yes, it was all Jim: the historian, the host, the guest, the devoted husband and father, the faithful friend. But something—what?—must be missing.

I didn't think it was just another case of a small-town boy who couldn't cut the mustard in the big city: that wasn't why we were bringing him home, over the mountains, now. In some ways, I had always thought Jim something of a loner, maybe even something of an actor. And by that I don't mean that he was fundamentally insincere, even false but rather that he was always on stage, in many roles—a meeter and greeter, a born showman (not a showoff), a born facilitator, one of those who, wherever you find them, always help to forward the cause of life. And I thought of an English actor friend (a very gifted comedian) who had once remarked, "Sometimes after a performance, when I come back to my dressing room, I'm almost afraid to look in the mirror for fear I won't see anybody there. My God, if you had any personality of your own, you wouldn't be a bloody actor in the first place!" And, as I said, he had been a very gifted comedian: he could make other people laugh their heads off. But he himself had been one of the saddest people I had ever known.

Now Harry, the doctor, speculated that perhaps, in Jim's case, there were medical problems none of us knew about; Linda wondered whether he hadn't died of an overdose of domesticity (had he really liked being married all that much?). I had the eyes and ears God had given me, and I wondered privately whether they were not both right. There were terrible things in the air these days, terrible states of mind and body, and perhaps it had all been too much for Jim. And maybe he didn't have the resistance to "throw it off," maybe he wasn't much of a survivor anyway —another casualty of the modern malaise. Had he been too easy-going for his own good? Could he look whatever might have been the truth about himself and his life in the eye? And don't forget the world he and I had both come out of. You didn't say all you thought, you didn't tell all you knew, and shame was often king of the universe. And despite the floods of talk that surrounded you on every side, your life was often full of the things you couldn't say, not to anybody in this world. And certainly not to the kind of people we had both come from.

I knew that at once when we stopped by the family residence en route to the old cemetery where Jim was to be buried after a graveside service. There were his parents—"older" when Jim was born, like my own; and he too had been an only child. There were a couple of aunts and uncles on hand and of course scores of cousins, all substantial, mostly well to do people—real *folks* as we say down here. And just what I would have expected. And I could tell none of them, fine as they were, had horizons much broader than the town itself. But they had loved Jim and were as grieved and puzzled as anybody else now. No, you couldn't rattle any skeletons in the closet around them: they would be only hurt. You'd have to keep it all to yourself. And all they could offer was "Perhaps he's at peace now, God bless him." And I thought, yes, I hoped so too.

At the cemetery there was a sizable crowd, and the Episcopal service was read, with Carol and the two daughters sitting beside Jim's parents. You could ask yourself of course whether Jim was not one of those who never should have married, but then in that case what about the two pretty teenagers? Carol had presumably gone on with life now; I had even heard she was dating a good solid accountant. And maybe that was what she had really wanted all along. What had Jim wanted—different commitments, different affections even, another stage to play on, a new mirror in the dressing room? Had he run out of encores? Like everything else, it was all a great puzzle. And who really knew what was right for anybody else anyhow? In any case, they—we—were all still here, but not Jim. And my eyes filled with tears.

I looked away from the grave: I just had to right then. And I saw an old-fashioned Southern cemetery—the sort I'd known all my life: dogwoods, azaleas in bloom, magnolias of course, even some graves of Confederate soldiers over to one side. And I thought about my grandfather, who had also died in the springtime. He was a survivor all right: yes, he was a Virginian who had been at Appomattox and had seen his world collapse around him but he had come out to Tennessee afterwards, met and married my grandmother, and never looked back. And he had taken hold and raised a fine family in the bargain. Why couldn't Jim have done something like that? Just for a minute my thoughts turned ugly, turned angry: if I could have gotten my hands on him, I would have liked to spank him hard. Why hadn't he put up more of a fight? How could he do all of us that way, all of us who loved him?

But then I heard the minister speaking "a few words" just before pronouncing the benediction. Thank God the Episcopal Church didn't go in for the sort of eulogy-cum-memoir of some churches. But perhaps this man thought, considering the circumstances, the restrained Prayer Book service might seem cold and unfeeling. So he paused briefly to note that Sunday would be Easter Day itself, the Feast of the Resurrection, which of course nobody could ever really understand. But whatever the Resurrection meant, it was some sort of *raising up*, and every time we were *raised up* from sorrow or defeat and enabled to go on with our lives, we experienced a "little" resurrection, which naturally pointed toward the "great" Resurrection itself. And maybe that was what it was all about. All very correct of course, all characteristically Anglican and understated but pretty good, pretty accurate, I thought. And nobody was ever likely to put it better, at least for most of us.

Afterwards we filed by and shook hands with the family, then went on back to Jim's parents' house for the routine after-funeral lunch, with of course enough food on hand to feed an army, all sent in by friends and neighbors, with tons of fried chicken and country ham. And talk, even laughter became general, with reminiscing by family and old friends who hadn't seen each other for some time—perhaps not since the last funeral that brought them together. (My mother use to say that, in the old days, that was one of the chief functions of funerals—to acquaint you with your kinfolks.) Finally, those of us who had to go back into our lives began to talk of being on our way. But it was all looking to the future now—tomorrow, next month, next year. The dead had literally been buried and life would go on. What would Jim's life have been like if he hadn't done what he had done? We would never know, and it would be profitless to speculate. That too would be part of the past we had just buried. And yes, looked at that way, stone dead had indeed no fellow.

But there were other possibilities too. And I thought of my grandfather and the Confederate graves I had seen just that morning: *they* had thought it all worth dying for, yes, but only because they loved their lives so well. And I thought of the way we had all been remembering Jim, and especially all the laughter, both at the table and in our memories. Was that too all part of a *raising up*? And I wondered about it now as we drove back over the mountains all the way to Tennessee.

The Maxwell Girls

Everybody said the Maxwell girls were a sight. They lived down at Haleyville, six miles below Woodville, the county seat, on the way to Memphis; and their house, which had a big front yard with an enormous oak tree growing right in the middle of it, was right on the main street, which of course was also the highway to Memphis. The Maxwell girls were both of them over eighty years old; but no one would ever have known it, either from the way they looked or, certainly, from the way they acted.

Frances, who was the older of the two, really kept the house and said she was the "homemaker" of the family: she never had married so, she said, she had to do *something* or else dry up. And back in those days when she first realized she was going to be a "maiden lady," as she put it, that was the only career open to a woman—keeping house—or else teaching school; and she said she wasn't about to do that.

Carrie, the younger sister, was a rich widow who had been married twice—the first time to a young man down in Mississippi, where she had gone to teach after she got out of the Normal. But he didn't *have* anything, she said, and wasn't about to *amount* to anything: the trouble was, they were just children when they married and she was practically a child bride. To which Frances, if she was present, would add, in a stage whisper, "You were twenty-five if you were a day." But anyhow Carrie and the young husband separated; and she married again, this time a much older man named Mr. Lucilius Long, who owned a big plantation down in the Delta, where she spent a lot of her time collecting antiques. And they were very happy, as far as anybody knew, until he died years later and Carrie came back home to live with Frances.

They also had an old bachelor brother, Marshall, who looked after their farming interests, which constituted the main Maxwell property, when he wasn't shut up in the back bedroom dead drunk. But when he was up and about, you could see him riding out to their farm every morning on the old mule he kept in the barn behind the house (the Maxwells had refused to tear down their barn even after they got a car). And the reason he rode a mule rather than a horse, he said, was that the mule didn't know but one thing to do and that was to go out to the farm and back so he himself never had to give it a thought whereas a horse might get *ideas*. (And of course if Marshall had a hangover, the mule would go right on to the farm regardless.) Anyway, that was almost all anybody ever saw of Marshall—going back and forth to the farm on the mule. But visitors to the Maxwell house lived in a state of delicious half-anticipation, half-terror that Marshall would suddenly emerge from the back bedroom in they knew not what state of intoxication and do something *perfectly awful*.

But to hear Frances and Carrie tell it, Marshall was the sweetest man that ever lived and the most gentlemanlike, though to a few intimates they would sometimes allude, in a dramatic whisper, to "poor Marshall's unfortunate habit," which again, unless you had the facts of the case, could have meant *anything*. But it wouldn't have taken much to shock Haleyville: the people in Woodville (which was twice the size of Haleyville) said it was the sort of place where you could spend a week (or feel like you had) in one Sunday-afternoon visit and the most exciting thing that could ever happen was for a petunia to bloom in the middle of a bridge game and there wasn't anything but widows and old maids down there anyhow and a real, live man who *was* a man, unlike Marshall Maxwell, would certainly never let the sun go down on him in the city limits of that place.

And really, that was what seemed to set the Maxwell girls apart. They loved Haleyville and said they couldn't imagine ever living anywhere else, but they seemed to delight nevertheless in providing the homefolks with plenty to talk about. And this was particularly true after Carrie had "lost" Lucilius, as she put it (Marshall always called him "old man Long" and Frances sometimes referred to him as "one of Carrie's antiques"), and come back home to live. Then a few years later Marshall himself died, more in self-defense, some people said, than anything else. So Frances and Carrie had a clear field then for their combined operations.

They had both aged well, with iron-gray hair and aristocratic, high-bred features—the kind of women that you never could have called pretty but that looked better, the older they got. And they had both kept their figures. So when they got all dressed up, they looked like *somebody*, people said. And they loved to dress up, to entertain and be entertained.

The thing was that though Carrie said she had altogether retired from the romantic side of life after she lost Lucilius, Frances still had a hot and heavy romance going, when she was well into her seventies, with a man named Ivan Currie, who was a well-to-do landowner out in the county but was young enough to be her son. And every Sunday night of the world he would take her out to dinner in Memphis or in some other less ambitious place if they didn't want to drive that far. He had lived with his mother, Miss Sallie, out at the old home place (big two-storied antebellum house) ever since his father died; and Frances said that was the reason she and Ivan couldn't ever marry: he couldn't—or wouldn't—leave his mother. But some people said the more fool she: Ivan Currie wasn't about to marry *anybody*. And after Miss Sallie finally died, Frances said it was too late then; and anyhow, if she and Ivan ever married, they would just settle down into "old married people" and all the bloom would be taken off their romance. And this when she was eighty!

A lot of people thought that Frances tried to keep Carrie in the background; and when you went to see them, she did most of the talking, never allowing Carrie to take a very prominent part in the conversation. And some people thought that was because she had always been jealous of Carrie for having not one but two husbands—and one of them a rich old man at that. And Carrie had had her own "plantation home," as Frances called it, down in Mississippi while *she* had had to stay right there in Haleyville and keep the home fires burning for both Marshall and herself. Other people said, no, that wasn't the case: Frances didn't want to marry any more than Ivan did, she preferred the arrangement just as it was. There had been a time, though, back right after his mother died, when Ivan had gotten involved briefly with a new beauty operator who had just come to town; but Frances had just stepped in and firmly put an end to that. Really, people said, he was probably grateful to Frances for doing so: he didn't want the rhythm of their Sunday nights interrupted any more than she did. They were each other's *social security*, in every way, and that was the way they wanted it.

Were she and Ivan more than just sweethearts, were they real lovers, people asked with raised eyebrows and bated breath. People in Haleyville (and in Woodville too, for that matter) never quite knew. Some people said of course they were: he was a man and she was a woman and, after all those years, what else could you expect? But other people said Frances believed in *romance* more than she did in *passion* and they wouldn't be a bit surprised if, after all that time, she was still, *ah-hem*, a maiden lady. This opinion shocked the first set of talkers as being more worldly, more daring, really, than their own brave willingness to face what they thought were the facts of life. But the fact remained that nobody ever knew for sure about Frances and Ivan, and that may have been just the way that she, especially, wanted it. O, she would refer to Ivan sometimes as her "sweetie" or her "boyfriend," which, at her age, might seem ludicrous coming from anybody else; but somehow Frances could get away with it because of her own love of the dramatic and her ability to make it acceptable to everybody else. O, she was a real cutter all right!

Disdainfully and of course with a full and appreciative audience, she would dismiss Miss Mattie Bates, "that old woman" (younger by several years than she was herself) who owned the property next door, as an *old hussy*, though she *was* locked up in a nursing home now and not in her right mind and on top of that still writing letters to her husband that had been dead for twenty years, because Miss Mattie's sewage was backing up onto her own side of the fence. And with great drama (and ill-concealed delight) she would regale her listeners with an account of the time Frank Clement, who was running for governor of Tennessee, made a speech in her front yard under the big oak tree (with her permission of course) and she sent out a monogrammed silver pitcher of ice water and a silver goblet for him to drink out of but never appeared herself because, she said, that man was so good looking, she was afraid to trust herself with him in her own front yard!

Or again, she would dramatically (and almost with gestures, as though she were giving an old-fashioned elocution "reading") recollect the circumstances of her cousin J. B.'s losing his first wife, Marian, in the terrible "flu" epidemic of World War I. She herself had been right there when Marian died, she said. (Of course J. B. had gotten an emergency leave to come home from the camp where he was training to go overseas.) But after they had prepared Marian's body for burial, they couldn't get the coffin upstairs to her bedroom because the staircase was too narrow. So J. B. had to bring Marian's body downstairs in his arms to put it in the coffin, and she would never forget that sight as long as she lived: it was the most pathetic thing she had ever seen. But then she would turn on her audience and explode, "And then J. B. had the nerve to go and marry that little upstart from out at Double Springs, Ida Nell Harrison— born white trash and still white trash—that always dyed her hair with what looked like stove polish, just six weeks later—said he was 'lonesome' and wanted to leave *somebody* behind him when he went 'across.' And every one of us could have killed him right then and there. And all of it on top of that memory of him bringing Marian's body downstairs too."

Carrie was always in the background when Frances was holding forth at home. People thought she was just too well mannered to interrupt Frances during one of her monologues; and perhaps she felt a little sorry for Frances, who had never been married while she herself had had two husbands, whom Frances occasionally pretended she herself couldn't tell apart, just to annoy Carrie. On the other hand, when Frances had said something particularly outrageous (or seemingly so to the Haleyville audience), Carrie would often look at the listeners out of the corner of her eye—and with a knowing little gleam too—as though to indicate that yes, she knew what was going on but wasn't going to do anything about it: she knew that Frances was all too aware of, indeed was perhaps working at being a legend in her own time. And yes, she was even a show-off, perhaps even at times an embarrassment. But Carrie was content to let it be that way.

On the other hand, when the Maxwell girls got all gussied up to go out to a social function, Carrie would come into her own because then Frances had more or less to *behave* since they were in somebody else's house. And then she would entertain her listeners with tales of her married life down in Mississippi, such as recounting the malapropisms of her neighbor, old Mrs. Allison, who after all these years could never get things straight and still referred to a "combine" on her plantation as a "concubine." Or else she would talk about coming back to Haleyville after her divorce years ago for a brief visit and finding that she, along with the postmaster's daughter who had "crossed the line" and thus "had a baby she wasn't supposed to," were regarded as the Scarlet Women of the town. Or, with something like tears in her eyes, she would recount the last sad days of "poor Lucilius" and how he had had to have an operation for prostate trouble ("they say every third man has it," she would whisper) and the doctors had cut too deep and so for the rest of his days he had had to wear a sort of diaper. And she would shake her head sadly as if to grieve over the indignities of life but also at the same time look amazingly as though she was going to *wink* at her listeners! At any rate, she implied, *she* was still here—and in business too!

Frances of course couldn't compete with that: she had never had a first marriage, much less a second. So for once she had to take a back seat. And that may have been why, about the time she had turned eighty, she quit "going out," as she said. (The Sunday nights with Ivan Currie were the only exception.) She said when anyone was her age, she could do as she pleased; and, if anybody really wanted to see *her*, he could come to her house, where she would receive him with open arms, providing she wasn't working out in the yard (still squatting down like a sixteen-year-old, to trim her flower borders) or back in the kitchen (she made the best watermelon-rind pickle you ever tasted—or smelled) or playing on her little electric organ, which she said she often did at six o'clock in the morning, when she woke up and couldn't go back to sleep. (She usually favored romantic selections from the early years of the century: "Ah, Sweet Mystery of Life" and "At Dawning" were often two of her choices.) So it was best to call first to find out whether she was "receiving." And if she was, the visitor could be assured Frances would tell him to come late in the afternoon, when she would offer him a little "refreshment" (which meant a drink to the few souls in Haleyville who drank at all). And then she would greet him at the door, she and Carrie both attired in something like very elegant negligees, probably the modern equivalent of the Edwardian tea gown. And he would be invited back into her "boudoir" (another word Haleyville found it hard to swallow) which was her bedroom and private sitting room combined. And then the performance would begin.

One young man (and the Maxwell girls always liked young men) who came to call with an old friend of theirs was greeted with "Why, I knew your mamma and your daddy before you were ever even thought of, and you look just like both of them," whereupon she kissed him on both cheeks as if to open the audience. Later on in the visit the young man idly asked what was the history of an old fan, framed and hanging on the living room wall. And Frances replied, "Why, that's a fan my lovers used to fan me with when I was quite a young girl. And see—the reason it's so tattered looking is that I made them so nervous, they almost tore it to pieces!" The young man was duly ensnared of course and remained her willing listener for life, whenever he could wangle a visit.

Everybody of course wondered which of the Maxwell girls would "go" first and then what the survivor would do with herself, they had been a "team" so long. How could they perform without each other, complements as they always had been of each other's "acts"? As it turned out, there was no problem really because one day when they were in their mid-eighties, they were both killed instantly in a head-on collision on the way to Memphis. (Where else?) Carrie was at the wheel of her big old black Buick and of course driving all over her side of the road and everybody else's too, the way she always did. And they never knew what hit them.

After all those years the two of them had become something of a municipal institution, so of course there was a big turnout at the funeral. And there were some cousins over in the next county to inherit their property: they'd never been tight-fisted but, where money was concerned, blood was thicker than water for the Maxwells, just like anybody else. In any case, everybody said it was a blessing Frances and Carrie never had to get old—or at least *act* old; and it was certainly much better for them to "go" like they did, taking their entire "act" on into the next world in one piece, still together, still a team, after all those years.

A Sweet Touch

Everybody in town thought it was a shame that Arthur Reynolds didn't go on with his music: he had such a sweet touch, they always said. In any case, he certainly ought to have gone on and "graduated" in piano, which meant at least majoring in music when he went off to college. But then of course that word could cover a multitude of endeavors: one of my aunts even referred to her son's completing his officer's training in the Air Force during World War II as his having "graduated" from the air. But whatever the context, it meant that you had more or less thereby been *finished* (almost like young ladies used to be in boarding school) and had learned everything there was to know about the subject. Whether or not you really "went on" with it was up to you and what you did with it in later years. In Arthur's case, would he try to be a concert pianist or would he just settle for being a church organist? If all else failed, would he still choose it as a career even if only to teach? That's what they more or less meant by the phrase. But whatever the case, "going on with your music" meant that you would be serious about it and not just put it aside as a luxury you were through with—had "graduated" from and had nothing else to learn there.

And Arthur was very talented, there was no doubt about that: he begin taking piano lessons even before he started to school. And he never settled—or his teacher, Miss Katherine Read, never settled—for any of that "Fairies in the Forest" sort of stuff for him to play. Why, he was playing Bach inventions and Czerny exercises before he was out of the third grade. And he loved it all too. Once I even heard him say, after he was in high school, that Bach's music was, like mathematics, simply inarguable and that if you could master the discipline of Czerny, well, then you could play anything else you wanted to, and whenever you wanted. It would just more or less play itself then. And that seemed strange—coming from a teenage boy. I really didn't know all that much about music, but I remember thinking he was much too young to know things like that. But then in some ways he was like a machine that way. I always wondered if he really *knew* what he was playing, did he understand it? Of course he hit all the right notes at the right time, but what did they mean to him? Maybe he just needed some age on him, but I wondered what he would make of Debussy and Ravel, to say nothing of Mozart, composers I noticed he didn't often play. The romantic repertory was certainly his for the taking of course, and he cascaded brilliantly through Chopin and Brahms, to say nothing of Liszt and, later,

Rachmaninoff. But sometimes I thought it was more dazzling sound than it was music and wondered where it would finally end.

But I'm getting ahead of myself here. Arthur was an only child—and born late in his parents' lives too, when they were both middle-aged. And I was never sure whether they knew just what to make of him, much less what to do with him. With no brothers and sisters and what cousins he had so much older, there was hardly anybody around for him to play with either when he was growing up. Maybe that was why he seemed to know things he ordinarily might be considered too young for: maybe that was why he always seemed out of step with either generation. On the other hand, in some ways he had no age either; he just more or less blended into the background wherever he was. But right now I still think of him as the rather chubby little boy sitting in the corner listening to all the grownups talk. I never thought he seemed particularly lonesome though, just alone. And I sometimes wondered what his thoughts were. Was he listening to every word the grownups—largely his parents, his aunts and uncles—said, storing it all up for future reference? But what sort of future reference? He didn't have any particularly close friends among his schoolmates to tell such things to, I imagined. And indeed, would they have even been interested? Incidentally, I should have told you in the beginning that I was his teacher in the fifth grade, and of course I had known his parents all my life. So I had a particularly good vantage point to observe all this from. And I had long ago discovered that if you just kept your eyes and ears open and your mouth shut, you could learn a good deal as you went through the world.

But I always wondered what his parents and all the rest of the family made of Arthur. Did they think he was a child prodigy? Did they think his musical talent would make him "too big" for Woodville and he would have to go somewhere else to earn his living? I don't know that they ever said much about it to him or anybody else. But as he grew up, a lot of people around town were certainly beginning to wonder. What sort of future could there be for him in a small town like Woodville? The Reynolds family were in comfortable circumstances, but they certainly weren't rich. And they couldn't support a sort of "musician in residence" just to have around the house. And somehow I didn't believe Arthur much wanted that either, though of course he never said much about such things. But then he never *said* much about anything. And indeed, with all those adults, some of them beyond middle age now, talking, he really didn't have much of a chance. But what I now know he must have been doing much of the time was turning into a first-rate listener. And I can tell you there are few enough of those around at any time. As an old friend of mine who was a great traveler used to say, "Nobody ever really wants to hear about your trip; they just want to tell you about theirs." And by and large, that's true.

But anyhow Arthur went on and gave his "certificate" recital at the end of his senior year in high school, with Miss Katherine playing the "orchestral accompaniment" on a second piano when he undertook the Mendelssohn G Minor Concerto. And there were a good many other pyrotechnics on the program too: Chopin's "Winter Wind" etude, even Liszt's "Mephisto Waltz." And everybody agreed that he was the best musician Woodville had ever turned out: why, they said, he could just make that piano talk! But what was he going to do now? Nobody knew.

But as it turned out, Arthur did. Because he went off to college that fall; and just before he left, he told a number of friends he was going to major in English and hoped to teach some day, maybe even be a college professor. And that knocked everybody off the Christmas tree, I can tell you. Yes, we all knew he was smart; and I knew, from teaching him, that he was a great reader with a very vivid imagination and great ability, at least in class, to communicate his enthusiasms to other people (and really, what else is teaching all about?). But no, not even I had reckoned on that as his chosen career. And certainly, I don't imagine Mr. and Mrs. Reynolds had either. But then to them I always thought he seemed more like an exotic hot-house plant than a real live son. But I don't want to do them an injustice either. Really, how could they—or anybody else—have known otherwise? As I said, he never talked much; but he obviously did a powerful lot of listening. And the Reynoldses were all great talkers, even performers. Mr. Reynolds himself was one of five brothers who all lived there in that one county and saw each other nearly every day of their lives, and their fund of old family stories was very large. They were all amusing people of course—what we call "good company." And everybody enjoyed being around them.

But one thing nobody had counted on was that somebody else beside Miss Katherine Read, his music teacher, had gotten hold of Arthur now. And that was Mrs. Edney, who taught him junior and senior English in high school. And she never said much about him outside the classroom; but she did tell me once, at a teachers' meeting, that she had great hopes for him: he knew a story when he heard one and could tell a good one too. (And I thought, well, he had had ample opportunities to learn the art.) But what hopes did she have? And really, I never had thought about that: he had mostly seemed quiet and watchful to me, certainly in some ways a loner, always on the edge of the group but never quite in it. I had never thought of his being any kind of "center," any kind of drawing card except of course as a musician. And then he communicated only through his music or rather somebody else's music—and then just his own interpretation of that. But what kind of stories did he have to tell, and how would they go along with his being an English teacher? And why hadn't he gone on with his music anyway? Had he just decided that he didn't have what it took and that for every Van Cliburn there were hundreds who never got beyond giving piano lessons or playing for church? Or did he think maybe whatever music he had in him was of a different order from that of the keyboard, the harmony of words? And was that what Mrs. Edney had helped him to see? It was all something of a mystery, to say the least.

Well, of course I just more or less put it all on the back burner for a good while: after all, I had a new batch of fifth graders every year to think about and more or less push and pull into line. One student more or less from years gone by wasn't going to keep me awake at night. But every now and then I would remember Arthur Reynolds and wonder how he was doing: he had graduated from college, even had a doctor's degree now and was embarked on his teaching career at a state university in the Middle West. And I had heard that he was getting some kind of reputation as a scholar of Renaissance literature. And all very highfalutin, it sounded, and not what any of us had expected. I had heard he had even sold his piano but of course continued a great music lover, never missing a concert on his campus if he could help it. But I suppose I still thought like a lot of other people in Woodville: it seemed a shame he hadn't gone on with his music. And yes, he had had a sweet touch.

Well, we found out before too long what he had been doing all those years besides publishing monographs on Shakespeare's sonnets and such like. Because about five or six years later (Arthur has just turned thirty) a very reputable New York publishing house announced that it was going to bring out a first volume of fiction (a collection of stories) by a new Southern writer, Arthur Reynolds, that would be set in a small town and deal with the townsfolk and the community, indeed something like the ones "Mr. Reynolds," as they called him, had grown up in the middle of, though of course the announcement hastened to add that in no way was it all to be construed as autobiography. And that of course set all Woodville by the ears. Had Arthur written about any of *them*? Had he "told all" about various delicate matters from the deep dim past, like the time Carrie Sue Henderson had called off her wedding to John Andrew Parks on the very day before it was to take place and nobody ever knew why or like the time the bank failed and several of the town's most distinguished citizens (including a Sunday School Superintendent) had had to spend several years as guests of the U.S. Government at the federal penitentiary in Atlanta? Would the skeletons be heard to rattle in everybody's closet? And what had that *child* been up to all those years anyway when everybody thought he was just sitting there listening to them talk? Had he been planning it all even then? And what about his piano lessons and his sweet touch at the keyboard? Where had all that gone to now? This, to say the least, wasn't the Arthur Reynolds they thought they knew.

Well, there wasn't anything anybody could *do* about all this. Mr. and Mrs. Reynolds were both dead and gone now and most of the aunts and uncles too. And people thought that might be a good thing: at least they wouldn't be around to be embarrassed, they wouldn't have to *explain* anything. And if Arthur had betrayed the town and its citizens, they at least would be spared that shame. But then word got out that the town library, housed appropriately enough in an antebellum "mansion" right off the Square which old Mrs. Parham had deeded to the town before she died because none of her children wanted to live there after she was gone (and she said she wasn't going to spend any more money on an old barn like that anyway: the next fellow was the one that could do all that), was going to give an autographing party for Arthur when he came back to visit in Woodville during his school's spring vacation. And of course everybody had to go, to see Shelley plain if nothing else, I suppose, and also maybe quiz the now "famous author" about the originals behind the characters and the stories themselves. And I had only one regret: Mrs. Edney had died several years before, so she wouldn't be there to savor the moment. And that's exactly what she would have done: *savor* it, whether good, bad, or indifferent. Because I had known her well enough to know that she had had enormous gusto for just about everything life had to offer and it would all have been grist to her mill. (Was it something like that that she had passed on to Arthur? Or maybe he already had it and she just made him realize he had it?)

But anyhow the great occasion all turned out to be rather anticlimactic. Naturally, I was right there to see and take in my two cents' worth. And certainly I wanted Arthur's signature on the copy of the book I had already bought (and read). It had been getting good reviews too: *The New York Times* called it a "promising debut" and said the stories themselves were "extremely well crafted," and one of the Midwestern dailies said the author had a very good ear for dialogue, perhaps it was no accident that he had begun as a musician. Of course the Memphis papers didn't take any notice of it one way or another: maybe they thought they couldn't afford to show enthusiasm for anything in the arts produced by somebody that close to home. In any case, my own experience in the world had long ago taught me that, in general, you needn't ever expect your own to take care of you.

But in some ways the book itself was all a let-down. O yes, some of the characters I thought perhaps you could identify. And of course it *was* extremely well written; and yes, you could tell the author had learned to listen long and well. But you would have been disappointed if you had expected to see all Woodville there only thinly disguised. Because the characters weren't the real live people the biographer would have written about: I had sense enough to see that without being told. But it was what those characters might have turned into in Arthur's head. It was what he had *made* out of them—and out of the town—inside himself. That was what the book was about, its shape and its form, maybe even its music. And I heard him give some kind of retort courteous when one of the good ladies for whom he was signing a book—Miss Ola Kate Evans, always bold as brass like all the Judsons, which was what she had been before she married—asked him when he was going to put *her* into one of his stories. And he simply smiled and said, "Why, I couldn't possibly do you justice." And everybody beamed appropriately: he had done the gracious thing. And I wondered whether I was the only one there with sense enough to get the double edge to his remark. He suffered a few more fools gladly before it was all over: things like "Now if I had just had your education, I could have been a writer too" or "I've got the funniest story you ever heard about my Uncle Jake but I need somebody to write it up for me. . . ." But Arthur never forgot his raising; he was always the gentleman.

The line of those waiting to have their books signed was a long one: nobody wanted to be left out, I suppose, whether for praise or blame. And I had to wait some time to get up to the table where Arthur was signing away. But when I did, I didn't have to wonder whether he would recognize me after so many years. He looked up and said right off,

"Why, it's Miss Elizabeth, my wonderful fifth grade teacher that made us all learn American geography and used to read Uncle Remus to us after lunch every day!" But when I asked why it was those particular things he remembered, he said, "Maybe it was you who got me started as a story-teller—that is, of course after I had heard all the folks in my family tell all their tales." And of course I was flattered and replied, "Now Arthur, don't lay it on too thick. How can you possibly say such things, though of course I *do* love to hear them?" And he said, "Well, my students certainly don't know their geography, much less anybody else's; they don't seem to think it matters where anybody is *frum*. But one way or another fiction has always got to have a place to happen in. And—and Woodville—certainly gave me that. And if you know all the devilment Uncle Remus's animal characters can get into—and get out of—I don't think much of anything real live folks can do will surprise you very much. Now what do *you* think?"

Well, that started all the wheels in my head turning around with a vengeance, I can tell you. What was he saying about his work, maybe even all the arts in general? Somehow I thought it wasn't just pleasantry: he was being quite serious. And I would certainly have to think about it all for a long time. But of course all I could think of to say right then was: "Well, Arthur, you didn't go on with your music, like we all thought you might. But there's certainly no denying that you still have a sweet touch."

What Papa Said
or
Sleeping under Two Blankets Every Night

When I was growing up, everybody I knew in my hometown went off somewhere in the summer except us. But my father said vacations were all foolishness, he had never had one in his life, and, besides, he needed to stay there and mind the store. And anyhow it was all money we didn't need to spend: I ought to think about my education, which was what we should be really saving for. Anyhow, why did anybody want to travel? Memphis was about as far as he ever wanted to get from home, and not very often at that. (And he had *been* to New York—on business—back before the First World War.) Furthermore, his mother, my grandmother, had never even been to Memphis, and she never rode on a train in her life. In the first place, she didn't have any money to travel on, and why should she *want* to travel anyway? All her family and friends lived right there in that one county.

But that was how I got to see all the new movies (back then we called them picture shows) before they came to the Dixie Theater in Woodville. Daddy would have to run down to Memphis in his pickup truck to one of the wholesalers some hot summer afternoon, and I would get to spend a couple of hours at Loew's State, where it really was twenty degrees cooler inside, just like the advertisements said, then meet him afterwards across the street at the Gayoso Hotel, where General Forrest's brother had ridden up into the lobby in an effort to capture Yankee General Hurlburt in a lightning raid during the Federal occupation of Memphis and where years later my parents had spent their honeymoon. But what was the point of air-conditioning if you didn't feel the cold? Daddy said he remembered the first electric fan he ever saw; and he wouldn't swap it for one of these newfangled attic fans that everybody was always bragging about because, they said, you could cool the whole house with one of them, especially during the night. But he wouldn't give you fifty cents for one of them, he said: they didn't even blow on you so you could *tell* you were getting cooler. And the day of houses with their own automatic air-conditioning was just not something he cared to even think about: you might as well be living in a department store, he said, or a mausoleum.

But practically everybody we knew was always going off to the Smoky Mountains or the Gulf Coast and sending us back postcards that said they were fine and hoped we were too and the weather was glorious and they were all sleeping under two blankets every night. And I hated and despised them all in my heart because I had never seen a mountain or the ocean and there we were almost on the Mississippi River and running the electric fans night and day (*oscillating* too—a word that used to fascinate me) but still burning up alive and getting eaten up by mosquitoes and not going anywhere or doing anything and not expecting to do so either. I even had malaria a couple of times, and that's the worst thing I know of you can have, not to kill you. But the mountains and the oceans remained for me—and still do—wonderful symbols of travel and trips and vacations and all sorts of glamorous things. And I spent a lot of time down at our depot watching the fast trains go by, north to Chicago and south to New Orleans, firmly resolving that one day *I* would be on one of them. (And years later it was the same in New York, when I would go down from Yale to see friends off for Europe on one of the great ocean liners; and, yes, one day it would be *me* walking up that gangplank.)

It used to worry me that my father never wanted to see such glorious sights and was so well content to stay at home with his own folks, like he said. I even thought sometimes he was proud of not traveling, as though there were some sort of inherent virtue in standing still or just taking a seat on the front porch for the rest of your life. (Or maybe, like Emerson, he thought traveling was a fool's paradise; and yes, some forms of it can be.) Perhaps my own desire to travel and see the mountains and the oceans and the great cities and sleep under two blankets every night was some sort of reaction against that.

My mother didn't seem so violently opposed to travel, but she *had* been to the St. Louis World's Fair of 1904 and put her finger in the crack of the Liberty Bell, which was on display there, and ridden the giant ferris wheel, where you rode in closed cars rather than on little benches open to all the elements and could practically feel death breathing down your neck. And years later she had taken an automobile trip through the Smokies, where she was sick as a dog from riding on the back seat until somebody realized she would be much better off up front. But this was not until after she had counted and recounted all the road signs along the way that warned "Prepare to meet thy God" or "Jesus is coming soon" every time she raised her head. So her own feelings about travel remained mixed, to say the least.

Anyhow, after I went off to college, I did do some traveling; and I loved it as much as I ever thought I would. I didn't know whether it was broadening me like people always said it would, but at least I thought I knew the folks back home—and myself—better than ever. And that was some sort of gain, because then you had something else to compare them with. And that was a something or a someone that didn't give a hoot in Hell about who your grandpa was or whether he was a bank president or a Sunday School Superintendent for forty years or whether your grandma's father gave her $10,000 to build a new house with when she married, which was practically the riches of Croesus in those days. But the main thing they couldn't have cared less about was what Papa, the ultimate oracle in that part of the world, said.

And that all has to do with the brand of folks that I'd put on the same level with the ones that had to go off and write back they were sleeping under two blankets every night. Because that was the one story of their lives and the only thing, really, that gave them importance or consequence—who Papa was and how much money he'd made and how respected he was in the community and so on and so forth until death did you part. Sometimes it was "Father" or "Pa" or "Papa," but it didn't make any difference; and the rose smelled the same by whatever name it was called. And there never had been anybody in the whole wide world like him for rectitude, probity, wisdom, prudence, piety, and of course, always, prosperity. Small-town aristocrats die hard, you know.

So it was two classes of people that I hated: the travelers and the backgrounders. And I realize now we'd call their respective ploys some form of gamesmanship, along with the strategy of nothing ever being as good as it used to be and food not tasting the same and no real quality anywhere anymore—what one of my friends calls the syndrome of "you should have seen the garden last year." They were all deriving their significance from something that had nothing to do with whether they themselves had any sense or any ability. In a way, of course, the groups were dissimilar: the what-Papa-saiders weren't much on travel because, after all, when you got somewhere else, the people there had never heard of Papa and didn't care what he'd said or when and where. And so, like Othello, their occupation was gone. Come to think of it, maybe the two-blanket-sleepers were their complements because that was all they did have in their lives: not much Papa and/or background. *They* were making it all alone—justification not by the works of others but by their own efforts, their own selves.

But neither one of these groups really knew where they were or you or me either because they couldn't put the at-home and the far-off really together. They didn't know that you really take your home with you wherever you go, that it shapes and defines your perception of other places, that you inevitably see the foreign through the eyes of home but, when you return home, your views on it have in turn been modified by what you've seen afar or abroad. And you can't really know the one without the other. But, in so doing, you go beyond the sleeping under two blankets and you get out of the range of what Papa said. You achieve your own identity then in a way you never could have before: you know where you are because you know where you came from originally, where you've been to since, and where you've returned to now.

The what-Papa-saiders are in complete command of the home terrain, just as the two-blanket-sleepers ride the whirlwind and direct the storm of sheer movement, what you might call irresponsible travel. But neither one knows where he is really because he has no other spectacles to look at it through. And they all of them keep repeating themselves, in one way or another wherever you go. The what-Papa-saiders, if they can ever be persuaded to travel, find that nothing they eat ever agrees with them and the hotels are never sufficiently clean (my own father said you could always tell that people who complained unduly about the food they ate "out" had all been raised on branch water, which is perfectly true, so maybe Papa wasn't such a fine gentleman after all); and the two-blanket-sleepers will always find out where you *haven't* been and then tell you that's the very place you should have gone first. And of course the food wherever you are now used to be good but not any more, now that things are not *normal*, which you suspect they never were in the first place. Usually when things were *normal*, Papa was alive, had plenty of money, and was going to take care of you for-ever-and-ever-Amen; that's what most people believe it means. In any case, whatever was *normal* was what you didn't have to worry about. But of course it's all relative. I even knew a man one time—a banker, of course—who thought things were *normal* when he could afford to keep a yacht.

I've spent a good deal of my life, one way or another, trying to get away from these two sets of folks, maybe even be revenged on them for what they did to my childhood and adolescence. Why? Well, they would have taught me to despise the really admirable qualities in my own home and the life we led there because they never, never could match up to the far off, whether in time or in space. And that's really what both these groups are: romantics, non-realists, or something of the sort—and both trying to prove something to you and perhaps themselves as well. Because for them it's always a Catch-22 situation—what you never knew, whether in space or in time, that is superior to what you have known, what you know now, where you've been, where you are now—your own self, your own home. And I think that's unforgivable.

Perhaps I shouldn't speak of them so bitterly had they not come so close to working their will on me: there was a time when I despised my own time, my own place because it *wasn't* what Papa said or it *didn't* have two blankets on the bed every night. But I think I did find out, after a while, that neither view was exclusively valid, that, in a sense, they complemented each other and a really sensible view of life at home or elsewhere had to comprehend, finally transcend, them both. Another way of putting it would be to say that history and geography should always go together. You really can't know one without the other. And only when you know them both can you be freed of the tyranny each is capable of exercising alone. Only then can you know yourself and finally possess yourself. Because, in the end, making a life work out of what Papa said forty years ago and sleeping under two blankets every night is really nothing but two different forms of involuntary servitude.

And who wants to travel through life like that?

As Clean as the Ten Commandments

When I was growing up, any infringement of the (unstated) rules of good taste where speech was concerned was strictly enforced by my mother, who would immediately take me by the hand, lead me to the kitchen, and wash out my mouth with castile soap—white with red veins throughout—which my father sold in his grocery and hardware store for a nickel a bar. (It was during the Depression, and I suppose that was the going rate then.) And really, it wasn't so bad—just mainly a sort of medicinal taste which lingered afterward and left you with the feeling that whatever you had done was somehow wrong and for some reason not in the best of taste. And so the punishment somehow really fit the crime.

Exactly what the criteria were for adjudicating the ineligibility of the word or words forbidden was often a mystery. The so-called four-letter words gave little trouble: I really didn't know what they were at that point. And my playmates and, later, schoolmates weren't much help either. Whatever the case, they mostly sounded like what grown people said when they were angry about something, but again it was hard to know exactly *how* angry they had to be before the words became really "ugly," which is how all such words were classified. Also the castile soap treatment was applied if you "talked back" or were "impudent" to one of your parents or some other eligible adult. And again, you weren't sure just how that distinction was made. Whatever it was, it somehow involved a questioning of adult authority but in a tone or attitude which showed a lack of respect for advanced years. So you had to watch your step, especially where matters concerning the human anatomy and methods of procreation and elimination were involved because you weren't always sure just what might be on the proscribed list. And yes, that did seem unfair.

I know now of course that neither of my parents was a real prude, and they certainly weren't squeamish about such matters. I think now they were mainly concerned with my having good manners, whatever the society and whoever was included therein. My mother was perhaps more inclined to something mildly risqué than my father. Like many other Southern men of his time (he was born in 1885 and unquestionably a real man's man too), he was fastidious about such matters. Yes, of course he knew all the words, but he apparently never felt the necessity for demonstrating his knowledge in public. And I never heard him use an obscenity in my life. Really, about the "worst" thing I ever heard him say—and more in exasperation than malice—was "the Devil!" But you could *imagine* the rest of what it might have been. And perhaps it was all the more intimidating for that very reason.

I've often wondered whether his mother, my grandmother, had something to do with this. More and more I've come to think that she was the real center of the family, while my grandfather was more of what my father called a "booster" than anything else. As a veteran of the Army of Northern Virginia, he may have felt that he had already been weary enough in well-doing in his time and there was no necessity for him to prove his mettle now. Which is to say that he was probably lazy and, as the son of slaveholders, used to being waited on and unused to much exertion, moral or otherwise. In any case, I've wondered why, though I've heard him quoted all my life—and he was apparently a real raconteur, with both Spottsylvania Courthouse and Appomattox in his repertory—he never seemed inclined to "hold forth" at the expense of the entire family. Everybody *knew* what he had done and where and when, and that was apparently enough.

But my grandmother was apparently very different. I think she must have known early in the day that the stability, if not the survival, of the family depended pretty much on her (after all, it was her small farm from which they drew their living) and she apparently was not one who ever knew much leisure. And somehow I don't imagine she much approved of *talk*, certainly not just idle conversation. (Perhaps she thought that's what got you into trouble.) So it was not only just a matter of female delicacy with her; maybe she just didn't feel she had the time. This may be just a speculation on my part, but nothing I ever heard about her— along with her many virtues and the adoration she inspired in her children —led me to think she must have been much fun. There just wasn't any time for that, and more than once my father hinted that she—and other women of her time and place—were often just *worked to death*. She was only sixty-two when she died, and they all talked about her as though she had been an old, old woman, whereas my grandfather lived to be ninety-two and was still up to snuff and a pinch over till the very end.

Indeed, so much was this the case that he remarried within a year of Grandma's death—her own widowed sister too—and of course it like to have killed his own children, who hardly ever spoke of it. (I never even knew of it until I was almost grown.) But it didn't last long, and in a very few years they were separated but not divorced. And she continued to bear his name for the rest of her life. I did notice once when I was out at the cemetery where she was buried (beside her first husband) that she was buried under his name and not my grandfather's. And whether that was due to remorse on the part of her children or jubilation on the part of my grandfather's, I didn't know. But I had the feeling that both sides were now content and quite willing to forget the brief interlude, and the less said the better.

Anyhow, I didn't grow up in an environment which encouraged "ugly" talk, whether it smacked of impropriety or insubordination. (Strange that it was that adjective they used to describe such lapses. Did they somehow think it was more genteel than a coarser word?) As was the case with most children then, I learned most such things from my schoolmates, along with a lot of mistaken information about the human body and all that went with it. If only my parents had known how much in the dark I still was, they might have behaved with greater tact and more information. But they were both very sensible people, and I suspect that if all of a sudden they had found themselves living amid the freedom and frankness which prevail today, they could have mastered their difficulties in due course.

But in their day it was thought just better to ignore what the French call "nature" and it would either go away or nobody would notice it; and only occasionally would my father, especially, take note that such things existed. (It was like the old joke about the Queen of Spain's legs: everybody knew she had them but it was thought indelicate to mention them. Or to put it into more everyday terms, my mother used to joke about the way she and others of her age had been brought up: women didn't have *legs*, it was implied, their shoes were just sewed to the bottom of their skirts!)

My father's approach to such matters was a little different. One of his favorite signs of approbation of a reference or a usage that might have been thought in questionable taste was to remark—somewhat offhandedly, "Why, that's just as clean as the Ten Commandments!" And then everybody could laugh with ease—and perhaps relief. And of course when you thought about it, there was nothing irreverent about it. (Why, I once heard Ann Landers caution a crowd of students against thinking of them as the "ten suggestions.") And our family had enough of the Methodist in them to know that the Christian religion could at times be a pretty salty business and there was no point in being ashamed of it. And of course there was implied in their attitude a strong sense of humor: none of them was either a prude or a prig. And they disliked such traits in other people. After all, the "ugly" things might on occasion also be very funny; and I don't suppose that Montaigne's observation that no matter how high a man sits, he still sits on his own bottom would have been lost on any of them. Surely it's all such things that are implied in that catch-all term "sense of humor"; and they all had that doubled and redoubled in spades. I've even heard my father say that he was afraid of people who didn't laugh, though, he added, he would have been just as afraid of people who laughed all the time. And I've even wondered sometimes whether he thought—without altogether knowing it—that laughter itself was somehow purgative and therapeutic and in its own way just "as clean" as the Ten Commandments.

For the Prestige

I don't remember him as a living person but I do remember his funeral, the largest "colored" funeral we had ever seen in our town. (When I was little, my nurse told me "colored" was what her people liked to be called—indeed, the then young NAACP had formalized the term as their own preferred term of race. Of course I also said "Negro"—and even "Nigra"—but never "nigger." And one of my aunts even said "darky," but she was a Virginian and that just seemed to come with the territory. In those days of course "black" would have smacked of the worst kind of racism, and "Afro-American" would have seemed academic, like some sort of exercise in sociology.) Anyhow the reason for all this ceremony was that he was a Confederate veteran: he had gone off to the war as his master's body servant. So his coffin was covered with the Confederate flag, and I learned later that he was buried with his campaign badges on too.

For years he had been the janitor at the white grammar school, where he was called "Uncle Lewis" by one and all—a courtesy title quite common for older Negroes in those days and I suppose we would say now an expedient to save us from having to say "Mr." (The older Negro women were called "Aunt" or "Auntie.") But anyhow this all must have been around the mid-thirties, when I was about four or five, and what I mainly remember was the funeral procession around the Square and being told that his coffin was covered with the Confederate flag, which I'm not sure that I had ever seen before.

My grandfather was a Confederate veteran too, and he was a Virginian who had been at Appomattox. And every year or two he and the other surviving veterans in our county would go off to the Confederate reunion, and Uncle Lewis would go along with them to keep an eye on them to see that they didn't overdo it though I can't imagine that they drank to excess or anything like that. But the late hours were something they weren't used to much any more, and sometimes they needed help with dressing and shaving, and so there was Uncle Lewis to help them out. I remember one time at the reunion the old soldiers were going to be bedded down in a school gymnasium on cots—no frills for them; and after all the South *had* lost so of course there wasn't much money around for them or anybody else, certainly not for their pensions, which naturally were paid by the states and not the federal government. Anyhow, when they were all getting settled down for the night in the gymnasium, some officious functionary said that Uncle Lewis couldn't sleep in the same room with them. But Pa, as we all called him, and the other old men weren't having any of that and they let it be known that if Uncle Lewis went, they would leave too. And that was the end of that. You didn't get on a high horse with old men who had once faced down a whole passel of blue-bellied Yankees, as they sometimes referred to them.

But the reunions were taxing on the old men: they always ate too much and kept later hours than usual, though as I said, I think the drinking was negligible. But Pa always got carried away by seeing all his old comrades in arms—talking to them, reminiscing, conjecturing all the "might have beens" and such like. So he didn't really look after himself properly. And one of the things he didn't have much time for was bathing, which he absolutely hated.

Whether this was all a holdover from his days with the Army of Northern Virginia I don't know; but every time he got back from the reunion, they would have a time getting him in the tub to wash off all the accumulated dust and grime of travel and late hours. One time, I remember, when he got back from the reunion (I think it was in Birmingham that year) he arrived down at Uncle John's house out from Memphis (Uncle John had a church on one of the circuits down there) and announced he was so sick he thought he was about to die. But whatever they did they mustn't tell Daddy and Uncle Buford, who had paid his way, because they would be extremely put out with him and might never let him go again. Uncle John wasn't home at the time, so Aunt Estelle promptly told him she was going to put him to bed and wash his face and hands and when Uncle John got home, *he* would give him a bath. And she said you would have thought Pa was about to be scalped. He didn't need a bath, he said: after all, he had only been gone three days and he could certainly wait till he got back out to Uncle Jim's place in the country, where he lived, and bathe there in the old washtub on Saturday night like always. And besides, he didn't have any clean clothes left to put on. But Aunt Estelle and Uncle John, when he got home, were both firm; so Pa did get cleaned up and Aunt Estelle got his washing done so he didn't have any more excuse about that.

Well, I don't know whether Pa and the other old men gave Uncle Lewis that much trouble at the reunion, but I suspect that like most black people of his time and place he knew how to handle them: you didn't argue, you didn't beg, you just sometimes forgot and went on your way. And anyhow Uncle Lewis let them do pretty much what they wanted to short of mayhem, and that was after all the best way to manage them.

And they thought the world of him too and treated him like one of the family.

Uncle John was the oldest of Daddy's four brothers and a Methodist preacher, but he was also a very good photographer on the side. (I'm sure he needed to augment his preacher's salary in any way he could too.) So we had lots of photographs of the old veterans all dressed up to go off to the reunions and, I also remember, all grouped around the Confederate cannon which had been brought up from Fort Pillow, the scene of Forrest's "massacre," which was down on the Mississippi not far from Woodville. And there was Uncle Lewis standing beside the cannon, along with the other old men, after they had gotten it placed in the courthouse yard and were ready to dedicate it as our county's official Confederate monument. He wasn't left out of anything ever.

Of course there were some things he couldn't do. I know there was one time when Pa was asked to sign an affidavit that one of the old men in the group really was a legitimate veteran: as a West Tennessean he had naturally ridden with Forrest but somehow the records were lost or mixed up or something and there was no "proof" that the old man was the real article. So Pa and another old man had to sign the affidavit, or rather Pa did because the other old man could only "make his mark." I remember it was the first time I had ever heard of a white man who couldn't read and write, and I was shocked.

What I suppose I'm getting around to here is some sort of statement or impression all over again of the closeness, the intimacy that existed in those days between Southern whites and blacks, certainly the whites who were used to having servants. It was usually the whites in the lower economic strata who were hostile or even worse toward them; certainly that was what I was always given to understand. And the first time I ever heard the phrase "po' white trash" it was used by my black nurse. But people like us, who had "had" things, my mother said, knew how to treat them; and again, it was all like one big family. Well, I know better now—the ways in which insidious exploitation took place, with prejudice not always well concealed, often indeed quite open, and of course with obvious condescension. But then in those days such servant-master relationships were not restricted to the American South; they were simply the way of the world and you made the best of it—certainly unless you wanted to rock the boat, which few people did then. So you could say that the town's attitude toward Uncle Lewis was a holdover from the *noblesse oblige* of antebellum days and as such it wasn't the best sort of relationship to maintain; but it seemed, for the time being, to work, and the future could attend to its own business in due course.

At any rate it never occurred to me to question the propriety of Uncle Lewis's having such an impressive funeral procession. Of course I didn't go to the service itself, but I gathered that many of Woodville's leading white citizens were there and some of them even spoke when called on by the black preacher, extolling Uncle Lewis as an example of the old times and the example he and his sort set for those now living. And I suppose today you would say they were turning him into a real Uncle Tom. On the other hand, they seemed all of them to look on him as some sort of member of the family, who very much belonged there—in his place of course. But it would all have been unthinkable without him. Everybody seemed to agree on that. And yes, it was all very much a community affair. That's the main thing I think of now. Would it be the same today, and would it be good or bad if it were? I've thought about that a lot.

And I suppose it was some such feeling as this, my very mixed feelings as I grew older and went away to school and then on to work in another part of the country, that prompted me to strike up a conversation with Uncle Lewis's daughter, Laverne, when I saw her in the post office the last time I was home. I hadn't seen her in a long time, but I knew that she had a son about my age and that she had taught school in the county for many, many years and also that she had had some several husbands along the way. In any case we greeted each other cordially, and I began to ask her questions about some of the other black folks whom I knew she would remember. And we became once more just homefolks to each other, belonging to the same place and time and not giving much thought to any of the usual conventions and customs, certainly the ones we had known in the old days. And she told me all about her recent retirement from the school system; and yes, she said she thought integration would finally work itself out very well in our county if people would just leave it alone and quit talking about it so much. However much color might divide folks, they were all of them held together by something much stronger than that and that was the pure D. unreconstructed Old Adam, which was the main thing we all had to worry about. And then she went on to tell me all about her son, Wilson, who had also spent his life teaching like his mother and father before him. (I didn't remember which of her husbands he was, but I thought any husband of hers would be quite all right and better than most people could manage now, the times being what they were.)

But then we got to talking about Uncle Lewis, and I told her about my remembering his funeral procession and how he used to go off to the reunions with Pa and all the other veterans. And I saw the tears come to her eyes as she observed that her own son, the same age as I, didn't remember his grandfather and how she wished he could. And I remarked that unfortunately, I didn't remember him personally, only the day of his funeral, but then that was characteristic of children and their love of drama. But I went on to say how much I knew Uncle Lewis had been admired and respected as a symbol of the old days and there weren't any like him left now, black or white. And she said no, she thought so too. And yes, she had been so proud of him and her family and what they had "stood for." And when they had recently organized a historical society in our county, she had been asked to join because, they told her, she was just an old Confederate like the rest of them, which she said gave her a lot of pleasure. And she told them she was indeed an old Confederate even if Uncle Lewis hadn't really been a soldier or even a "body servant" so much as a "forager," whose main job it was to steal as much food and equipment as he could from the Yankees: that was what he was really there for, to look after his own folks, black and white. And did I know one thing, she concluded: every time she had gotten divorced, she had always taken her maiden name back till she married again and if anybody wanted to know why, she was only too glad to tell them it was for the prestige, she was so proud to have been born who she was. And then I thought of Pa and all the other old soldiers, and I told her I knew exactly how she felt.

Anyhow, it wasn't long after that that I happened to see Wilson and he told me that he had recently retired from teaching—they were nearly all of them teachers in that family; and so he had just attended the annual reunion of the Sons of Confederate Veterans, which had met this time in Atlanta, and he had had a great time, with white folks, black folks, and the whole shebang. Of course there were no real veterans still alive, but their grandchildren and so on had had a great time talking about them all and recollecting the tales they used to tell. And his grandfather, he told me, had been in the Battle above the Clouds at Chattanooga, which they said now was a misnomer because it wasn't *clouds* they were above but just plain old mist or fog or something. But *clouds* naturally sounded more dramatic. Anyhow, I hadn't seen Wilson in a good many years, and he even reminded me that when he was young (he's only a year or two older than I am), he used to hear me practicing on the piano while he was mowing the yard of the folks next door. But I told him I'd just as soon he forgot that period of my life.

Anyhow he said he wanted to tell me about the big to-do at the reunion because of the whole uproar being made now over the fact that some of the former Confederate states still retained a facsimile of the Confederate flag on their respective state flags. And every group in the country that wanted to be disaffected or outraged or anything else was raising all sorts of Hell about it. And he said he knew Atlanta was supposed to be a mighty progressive place and leading the pack when it came to getting more and more reconciled with past, present, future, and God knows what else. But nobody was going to tell *him* what he ought to think about any of it. So when a right feisty newspaper man came up to him at the reunion and asked him what *he* thought about all the hullabaloo, especially since he was the descendant of a *black* veteran who had been more or less *forced* to bear arms for such an infamous cause, Wilson said he didn't know what the other descendants like him might say but his mother, Laverne, who was Uncle Lewis's daughter, had told him she hadn't ever seen anybody yet that could *force* her father to do anything he didn't want to. And he told his daughter he had more things to do with his time than to take notice of anybody, black or white, that didn't know how to behave better than the Yankees, who had the worst manners and talked the "ugliest" of anybody he had ever seen or heard in his whole entire life. And now as far as Wilson himself was concerned, he said it was all a mountain made out of a mole hill and he was absolutely *pissed off* with the whole thing and sick to death of hearing about it. And all the newspapers and everything else could certainly quote him on that.

And then he asked me what I thought about all the commotion; and I said that, as far as I was concerned, we were all of us, black or white and all shades in between, just good old Confederates together. And they could all quote that too and, by the way, where was the reunion going to meet next year? And when he said Richmond, I said that was just fine, and I would see him right there.

New Year's Eve

I was just visiting a cousin in Crockett City, but I had heard about the Fontaine sisters' parties for a good many years. They had three big parties every year—Fourth of July, Christmas Night, and New Year's Eve; and everybody in town went, old and young. And my cousin, Margaret Anne, had told me I really ought to go sometime: there was nothing else like them anywhere around there, she said. But when I asked her why, she said it all had something to do with the nature of the sisters themselves—Jennie Mae, the older one, and Lula Frances, the younger. But you always thought of them as a twosome, more like twins really; and you hardly ever saw one without the other. Indeed, some people couldn't even tell them apart.

But what was so different about them, I asked. Well, she said, their old mother, who had been a Poindexter, had never let them get married or leave home and had kept them right there under her thumb until she died a few years ago, aged nearly a hundred. Why, she never had let them have a real date with a boy or, if they did, they had to sit right there on the front porch where she could keep them under her eagle eye. And if one of them did go out with a young man in his car, they had to just drive back and forth, up and down the street, where she could see them from the front porch swing every time they went by. And yes, it was a long front porch—old antebellum house that had been in the family for five generations, white columns and all. But now that the mother was dead, the two maiden ladies went right on living there, just the two of them. And they were part of everything that went on in town.

That was the funny part, Margaret Anne said. "You'd think they would have just dried up right there after their mother died. After all, I always thought she'd sapped the life out of them; so with her gone, what would they have had to look forward to? She had been practically the only life they had, except for their parties. And until she died she even dominated *them*. She was usually seated in a big arm chair in the parlor, all dressed up, with her wig on and her teeth in, and you always had to go speak to her first before you took any notice of the sisters. But whatever you said, you never mentioned old age. She always said she was younger than her daughters."

"But do you know what they did after she died?," she went on. "They opened up a dress shop right down on the square and started carrying a nice line of clothes for ladies—not too fine for a small town like this but nothing tacky. And the main thing was that they took a new lease on life and sort of blossomed out. When I asked them about it one day, they said of course they could have just sat right there at home and folded their hands and looked in the mirror more or less. But this way, they could be out and about and mix and mingle and see folks. And that was what they *loved*. On the other hand, they're pretty hard-headed where business matters are concerned. I know I asked them one time why they didn't have more chairs in the store, and they said if they did, customers might take a seat and start visiting with each other and never leave. They didn't love folks that much!"

"It all sounds sweet and brave but rather pathetic to me," I said, "to think of them more or less emerging into an Indian summer like butterflies from a cocoon after their mother departed from the scene. Anyway, what was their father like?"

"O, they're not pathetic, anything but; you'll see. As for their father, he was an old-fashioned country doctor, and all of us went to him as long as he lived—a good one too and supposedly a first-rate diagnostician, they always said. And yes, I think he did loom large in the daughters' lives. I know Jennie Mae told me one time they still had all his medical paraphernalia stored up in the attic. But maybe he was always just too busy, too much on the go to take much notice of them, because I think their mother had them in hand almost from the beginning. Of course, with all the stuff there is in that house—I don't think they ever threw away *anything*—I used to wonder whether they might not have Dr. Fontaine himself tucked away upstairs. And somebody did tell me one time that after Mrs. Fontaine first died, Jennie Mae and Lula Frances used to go by the cemetery the first thing every morning and the last thing in the evening, on the way home from the dress shop, and tell her good morning and good night."

"Well, now, that's a good old Southern Gothic story for you," I said. "Really, you're just one jump away from Faulkner's Miss Emily Grierson that killed her lover and then kept him hidden away in an upstairs bedroom for the rest of her life." (I was an English teacher and didn't mind seeing the parallels between literature and life.)

"O don't get 'literary' on me about all this," Margaret Anne replied, amused but indulgent. "The Fontaines never were 'peculiar' or anything like that. (I suppose now we'd say 'kinky.') I think the 'girls'—as their mother always referred to them—were simply acknowledging their loss in a dignified and tasteful manner, nothing more. I know they've got white pansies planted all around her grave—and Dr. Fontaine's too. And anyway I think they stopped going by to 'speak' to her long ago. That didn't amount to anything. It was all just their way." And of course that was a phrase that more or less justified anyone or anything in the South that was "peculiar"—itself a wonderful catch-all word in that part of the world. Of course I'm Southern myself, but I went to school up north, then taught up there for some years, so you can say I have a double vision about it all. People like Margaret Anne do too, but they've more or less learned theirs by ear, you might say, especially from traveling. She's lived there all her life, in Crockett City, married there and buried there too. And now widowed and with no children, she can wander around and see the wider world a bit.

In any case it was Margaret Anne who always brought me up to date on the Fontaines when I went to visit. She had lived right down the street from them for most of her life; and yes, she "appreciated" them: she knew you didn't see their like just anywhere. Yes, she knew they were somewhat "set apart" from the main stream of things over there—living by themselves in that big old house, running the dress shop downtown too—yet she said nobody in the place was more "into" things. They went to every wedding and sent flowers to every funeral, and they knew everybody in town and vice versa. And I told her, yes, Faulkner's Miss Emily, by her very "apartness," became somehow community property because in that sort of place, where community was almost everything, your being somehow "outside" it made you more than ever "belong" to it. And was that somehow true of all self-appointed outcasts and loners? Look at Thoreau, I said. But again, Margaret Anne said not to get literary, it was nobody but Jennie Mae and Lula Frances.

But anyhow I never had been to one of the Fontaine sisters' parties, and I really should, Margaret Anne said. Everybody in town came, because they were an "institution," and for days ahead of time everybody that came in the dress shop would be invited and told to bring her folks. And I wondered why it all didn't get out of hand, where room was concerned, to say nothing of the expense. But Margaret Anne said never mind, I would see. And that's exactly what I did want. For one thing, I had never been inside the Fontaines' house, which, in addition to the white columns, had an appropriate name: Greenlawn. (Yes, it was set back from the street in a big yard.) So of course I wanted to see the show or the spectacle or whatever it might be. And I was staying with Margaret Anne over the New Year's holiday and could go to the party with her.

It was always called a party too, never an open house. Sometimes I wondered about that. And I even asked Margaret Anne what she thought about it. Well, she said, she never had thought much about it one way or the other; but "party" was more in keeping with the Fontaines because they always thought they ought to *entertain* their company, not just let the bars down and holler "y'all come" and devil take the hindmost. They *worked* at their parties, she said. And I thought for a moment of my mother, who when somebody once told her how beautifully she entertained but it was all so much trouble, replied, "Anything in this world that's good is trouble." And I wondered whether the Fontaines were of the same mind.

Anyhow, on New Year's Eve, Margaret Anne called to ask whether she might bring me along—her professor cousin, she said, who was homefolks but had still lived and worked up north among the Yankees. This party, she explained to me, didn't begin so early as the others because the climax didn't arrive till midnight. You could celebrate the Fourth of July most any time of day, and Christmas Night was just that and reserved for the grownups after the children had all had their Santa Claus and been put to bed. And that was when the family (all the Fontaines' connections from all around there in West Tennessee—Crockett City was only forty miles from Memphis—and of course all down in Mississippi) came and there was a Christmas tree with heirloom ornaments and all such. Really, of the three annual parties, New Year's Eve was the least colorful or exciting, Margaret Anne said, though it was the latest. But anyhow she called them and talked to Lula Frances, who answered the phone and screamed with delight when she heard Margaret Anne say she wanted to bring me along. "Why of course you must bring him. We've always wanted to meet such a distinguished man!" And you could have heard her all the way across the room. Margaret Anne said the Fontaines never did anything by halves.

So along about nine-thirty we got ourselves all dressed up and walked down the street and climbed the steps up to the front porch of Greenlawn and knocked on the door. I couldn't hear any talk or laughter or music, so I wondered whether we might not have come too early. But Margaret Anne said no, people came and went as they chose. And then the door opened and there they stood—the Fontaine sisters, Jennie Mae and Lula Frances, their hands extended in cordial greeting, smiles broad and beaming with sheer delight, and welcoming us in with "You're the first to arrive, and now we can really get acquainted with Margaret Anne's cousin before all the rest get here." Well, that wasn't exactly what I wanted, to be made something of a sideshow attraction. I was there to look and listen myself and didn't envision any other role as suitable for me under the circumstances. But that was the way when people, especially Southerners, first met "brought on" folks, I knew. Perhaps it was just a superflux of the fabled hospitality.

In any case, there they stood in floor-length gowns (their own merchandise from the Town and Country Dress Shop, as it was called?), their hair "tinted" with a heavy "rinse," and ready to perform all the honors of the house and the evening. Which in due course they did, beginning with the guided tour. First the front parlor, on the right, complete with ancestral portraits, including that of the great-great-grandfather who had built the house itself. (He was a big "planter," they said, and, on the side, since in those days "professionals" were so few and far between, an undertaker —and I wondered whether they might be conscious of their own play on words and also whether they might not still have *his* instruments on hand somewhere around the house.) And there were a square piano and a reed organ, faded crimson draperies at the floor-length windows, and a couple of pier-glass mirrors also almost floor-length. So far so good. But there was no roaring fire in the fireplace, just "gas logs" turned up full tilt. And the flowers in the dime-store vases were all paper, the framed "mementos" on the walls mostly Christmas cards from a few years ago. Stacks of music on the square piano but much of it thirties and forties popular songs—mostly saved from the sisters' own young ladyhood, I reckoned. Most of the furniture except for one handsome old secretary over in the corner was just standard small-town furniture store stuff. And I wondered what had happened to its predecessors.

I didn't imagine the ladies had very much ready money to hand; it was all beginning to look like "shabby genteel," a phrase not uncommon down South. The wallpaper was peeling, and the woodwork hadn't been painted in a long time. And over everything there hung the fierce heat generated by the small gas heaters, which seemed to be found in every room, and the heavy odor of the ladies' "body powder," as it used to be called—it came in small round boxes and in the old days no real lady would have thought her bath was complete until she had dusted herself liberally with "Evening in Paris" or Yardley's "Old English Lavender" after she had dried herself off.

Until that moment we had been the only guests in the house; but now —as we progressed into the dining room, which opened, through folding doors, out of the parlor—there were several middle-aged couples who irrupted into the front hall, full of laughter and high spirits, to join us. The sisters performed the necessary introductions somewhat vaguely, but of course in a place like Crockett City you always assumed that most everybody was kin to most everybody else and it really didn't make much difference. (Do you wonder that after all these years I still don't open my mouth to say *anything* until I've first looked around the room to see who's there and who's kin to whom?) And we proceeded on to the dining room and the refreshments.

I noticed that some of the new arrivals had brought plates of delicacies—candy, cookies, and such like appropriate to the occasion. But the food on the dining table (covered by a plastic "lace" cloth) was mostly ordinary sandwiches (I noticed the crusts hadn't even been cut off the bread) of cheese and tomatoes, perhaps even peanut butter. The punch bowl itself was not "ancestral," just a reproduction of Victorian plate, I thought; and it had what looked like mostly store-bought punch inside. I don't know whether it had been spiked, but there were some bottles of wine and "cold duck" on a table over in the corner. And candles in plastic holders everywhere. But the floor looked as though it hadn't been swept in weeks, and there was dust on most of the gewgaws on the mantelpiece—again nothing "historic" (I had been hoping for china dogs), just dime-store bric-a-brac.

The ladies kept disappearing into the kitchen from time to time, to fetch more food, more punch, but I didn't imagine that much more was needed. And I wondered what they would do with the leftovers. (Margaret Anne had whispered to me that she never *ate* anything at the parties, only just the goodies the other guests brought, and drank a glass of wine and that was all.) There were no flowers on the table, just artificial poinsettias and holly, but it was all very festive with conversation and laughter. Of course most of the guests, who kept coming in unannounced from the front hall, knew each other well and had probably seen each other only a few days before at another holiday revel; but that didn't keep them from resuming, sometimes even repeating whatever conversation they had been having at the time. And there was lots of talk of kinfolks and neighborhoods. Yes, all very Southern.

Margaret Anne had already told the Fontaines that we wouldn't be staying late: I had been on the road traveling and she herself was trying to come down with a cold. But of course they said we must stay till the new year came in on television at midnight—but New York midnight and not our own. Yes, of course it was Eastern time, while we lagged behind one hour on Central. But that was all some of the guests felt they could manage—age and health being what they were. So we simply *had* to stay for that, they said, when the electric ball descended on top of the skyscraper in Times Square and it was all official—at least for the East Coast. And besides not all the guests had arrived yet. And we *must* find somebody to play "Auld Lang Syne" on the square piano: they had a real simplified version available in an old book of songs. Of course they always sang "Dixie" too, just on principle. And then some time after the stroke of midnight (even if it was a sort of Yankee midnight) there would be fireworks out in the front yard. No, indeed, you couldn't let the side down and leave too early and, besides, last year at this very party there had been a proposal right there in that dining room: a young man had actually kneeled down and presented a diamond ring to his "sweetheart" —and been accepted too. And who knew what else might not happen in such a romantic old house at such an exciting time as New Year's Eve? Greenlawn had certainly seen a lot of history in its day.

And now one more batch of guests arrived—a group of high school students and some college students home for the holidays. And after some rather awkward introductions, everybody young and old relaxed on something like an equal footing. The young people were mostly the children or even grandchildren of the older guests, and I learned from some of them that the Fontaine sisters' parties were a tradition in the town for the young as well as the old and the young people expected to go to them too—if not as some sort of initiation ceremony or rite of passage, at least a sort of welcome to being full-fledged members of the town and community. (Of course they didn't *say* all that, but their meaning was clear. And they thought the parties were "neat.") And when I questioned some of their seniors, they said things like "O yes, I began coming to the parties many years ago myself; we all did. And now it wouldn't seem right—whatever the holiday is—without them. The Fontaines—and their parties—are simply fixtures here." The young people at first hung about somewhat hesitantly; but when they saw their parents and even grandparents participating in the revelry with such zest (mostly without benefit of alcohol too), they relaxed and more or less joined the group. And I remembered my mother's saying years ago that when you grew up, everybody was the same age. And I thought the room—and the guests—were an interesting study, in more ways than one.

From time to time I would have to take a breather out on the front porch: all the gas heaters and the body powder would get too much for me. And then before I came back into the dining room, I would wander around the other rooms—all "thrown open to the guests," as it used to say in the "society" write-ups in small-town Southern newspapers—and see what lay there. Across the hall from the parlor was of course the front bedroom. And it was a bedroom to end all such, with three Victorian bedsteads and a fine old wardrobe occupying most of the available space. And when I asked Margaret Anne why there were so many beds in one room, she replied that when old Mrs. Fontaine was alive, they all three had slept in that one room and in fact never seemed to use the upstairs to the house at all: she assumed there were more bedrooms up there. Whether it was economy or simply the desire for company that prompted their decision she didn't know.

Whatever the case, all available space in the house seemed to be utilized, and nothing ever seemed to be thrown away or discarded, whether genuine or junk. The bedroom walls bristled with photographs of (I assumed) kin, living and dead (and sometimes it was hard to tell the difference). And they were interspersed with lithographs of nineteenth-century landscapes and scenes from Scripture. Back numbers of fashion magazines (from the sisters' store?) were stacked in the corners. And again, on the dresser, on the mantelpiece bric-a-brac abounded. And I thought of the Collier brothers I had read about years ago in *Life* magazine, who more or less drowned under the immense piles of magazines, newspapers, furniture, clothes and God knows what else in their New York brownstone. What was it all about—an attempt to turn back the clock, to freeze time in its place, to hold on to whatever you found meaningful or important in your life? Was it all, as some people now might irreverently say, just some sort of security blanket? I never had known; some people just seemed to be turned that way, and particularly Southerners. And maybe it did them good. But whatever the case, I wished them all well.

The old year was fast waning away—or the New York old year, to be precise. And there were a couple of television sets running full speed ahead so everyone could see the crowds in Times Square and of course follow the descent of the magic ball, which symbolized the departure of the old year and the arrival of the new. But just a few minutes before the great moment arrived, the sisters disappeared into the kitchen and returned, dragging behind them a large cardboard box containing "party hats," which we all had to don. And to make the scene complete they even brought out noisemakers to signal the impending event. And dutifully, all the guests, of whom there must have been about twenty or thirty by now, put on the hats, took up the noisemakers and, you might say, girded up their loins for the main event. And in due course, as the ball completed its descent, they began their own ceremony right there, hats in place, noisemakers making their infernal racket, the elders some of them looking sheepish but the younger crowd, having lost their original diffidence, now throwing themselves into the spirit of the occasion. And the moment was duly celebrated. I myself got carried away, in the midst of it all, and, having already declined to "preside at the console" for the playing of "Auld Lang Syne," raised my voice in leading the same song and soon found all the others joining in, young, old, the whole lot. Yes, it was a magic moment.

The Fontaines must both have been well up in their seventies by now, I thought; but their gusto, their zeal for life must have been just as strong as ever. And I could see that the young people present somehow sensed that and now honored it in the two old women who were, after so many years, in some measure still childlike (not childish) and never afraid of appearing foolish, even absurd. And no, you couldn't condescend to them either. They, like the old house itself, couldn't be bothered with what was "in" or "out," what was stylish or what was tacky. They all had more important things to do—going on with their own lives, going on with life itself, in good times or bad, hearts and heads high, each year thus joyfully continuing to celebrate this exchange of the old year for the new. *They* weren't going to be like the Collier brothers. And maybe it was all of it their "thing," as we would now say, both for themselves and for the town.

At any rate it was something like this that I thought when I heard the next morning that, after most of us had left, it was the young ones, now their latest recruits, who had stayed on for the real, Central-time New Year's Eve an hour later. And it was they who had helped the Fontaines set off all the fireworks.

The Lock Box

The week after my mother died I had to go down to the bank and stand there, in the vault, while her lock box was opened in my presence and that of various bank officials. The prime consideration was withdrawing her will from the box so it could be submitted for probate, but also an inventory had to be made of the box's contents. Of course there were no particular mysteries about it all. My father had been dead for ten years, and I was her only heir, so her will specified (it had been made jointly with my father's) that everything was to go to me if I survived him. But it had been a long time since I had occasion to examine the box's contents, so I wasn't sure what might be found there after all the "legalities" had been accounted for—her will, the deeds to our house and some farm property, both her own and my father's.

I knew of course there wouldn't be much in the way of "valuables" there: mainly her only piece of "good" jewelry—a diamond solitaire—and my father's gold watch (the "Illinois" brand used by railroad crews because you had to take the crystal off to set it). But she had very little "real" silver—that is, sterling; and her china (the old-fashioned French Haviland pattern with the scalloped gold band, no longer available anywhere) and her crystal had been stored away in a rental facility during her long final illness, along with the few pieces of old furniture I had retained after I sold our house—her grandfather's walnut secretary put together with pegs instead of nails, an old linen chest that had been brought all the way from North Carolina "over the mountains in an ox cart," the old oak dining table and chairs my father and his brothers had all grown up "fighting around," as he used to say, and the doughty high-back rocker that had been his father's, the Confederate veteran.

She had worn her wedding band (made from her own mother's) during her illness, but it had somehow disappeared during the years of hospitals and nursing homes. And the only reason she had not continued wearing the diamond solitaire (an absolutely perfect stone displayed to the greatest possible effect in a Tiffany mounting with platinum prongs) was that I had insisted it was too valuable to do so under such circumstances. She had hardly ever had it off her hand before that, even when she was washing dishes: "Soap and water never hurt a good diamond," she always said and then, holding it up to the light, would add, "There are bigger diamonds in the world but none finer." She had bought it herself as an investment before she and my father were married, and it was one of her few vanities. Sometimes I would tease her about buying her own "engagement" ring, but neither she nor my father ever objected to that. In fact, I believe he was secretly proud of her for showing such resourcefulness: if at that point he couldn't afford to buy her such a gem, well, more power to her for having the spunk and the determination not to be without one and for having the sense to know a good investment when she saw one. (She was nothing if not *practical*: "mathematics was always my long suit when I was in school," she used to say. And when one of my cousins married a young woman who was so down to earth it was almost like she was drowning in quicksand, she gave her the highest compliment in her power: "when time comes to cut the head off, she's right there ready to do it.")

But that was about all there was in the way of "treasures"; the rest was, you might say, sentiment—and on the whole, mostly of my father's doing. Of course there was Grandpa's "parole" from the Army of Northern Virginia, signed at Appomattox Courthouse on that Palm Sunday in 1865, which made it clear that, as a "paroled prisoner," he was now entitled to return to his home (in Powhatan County) and remain there "undisturbed," which way of putting it had always fascinated me because I couldn't imagine anybody on God's earth even thinking of "disturbing" such a fierce old man who had a head as hard as a rock and an iron will to match. (One time in his last years he decided he must be rich since he never had *spent* any money, and it was useless for his children to dissuade him when he wanted to start writing checks so they were forced to just whisper in the bank's ear and hope for the best.)

Of course I was always afraid of him just because he *was* so old (he was ninety-two when he died and the last veteran in the county) and had a big walrus mustache, which had the same effect on me as Santa Claus's beard: I didn't know *what* might be behind it. But now I have his "parole" framed and hanging on the wall in my living room and of course proud for everybody to know he wasn't afraid to say *yea* or *nay* when the time came, though I don't think he was really one to harbor lifelong resentment when the Late Unpleasantness was over. He apparently just did what he thought he had to do when the time came, and he lost. You might say of course that he came from a nation of losers, but he remained always nonetheless proud because he thought he had lost with honor. (After all, he had seen General Lee riding down to give his farewell speech to his assembled troops, accompanied by tears as well as by hurrahs; and my father had once heard that "Great Commoner," William Jennings Bryan, speak from the rear platform of a campaign train, trying to persuade the electorate of our town to vote for yet another losing Democrat—Cox or Davis, I believe—who didn't necessarily think that those who supposedly "owned" the country were therefore entitled to run it.)

Two other keepsakes in the lock box were obviously of my father's own choosing—my first "baby tooth," which the attached card noted had been "drawn by his Daddy" when I was five years old, and a letter I had written Santa Claus, addressed to "the North Pole," when I was seven and somehow retrieved from the mail and passed on to my father by the post office. And perhaps each of these things my parents had chosen to put in the lock box was, respectively, characteristic of each one, even telling more about them both than they probably knew. My mother, with her respect always for "quality" and "reality," was represented by something that would last, would always be genuine, whether it was a diamond or, as in her own choice of clothes, *in style*, which, unlike *fashion*, was definitive and not subject to change and as good today as both yesterday and tomorrow.

On the other hand, my father chose more what I suppose we would call items of *sentiment*, not sentimentality, I should hastily add—those things which quite properly touch the heart in a straightforward, manly way, but permit little self-indulgence, something rare enough among Southern male WASPs. But he himself was never ashamed of tears: he would say that he was crying "for joy," for happiness and gratitude because of what God had blessed him with. And in later years I would always think then of what Lord David Cecil said about the Whigs in his fine biography of Lord Melbourne: "Happy creatures! They lived before the days of the stiff upper lip and the inhibited public school Englishman. . . . It never struck them that they needed to be inarticulate to appear sincere."

These then were the keepsakes, the mementos, the souvenirs the lock box held, some of them intrinsically valuable but others of little interest to anybody outside the family circle. And I believe my parents thought this was just as it should be. After all, my grandfather had been only a private in the War, and he had run off from school to join Hardaway's battery in the artillery. And there was no glamor to any of it, just firm conviction and a stout heart.

But who really wants—or needs—to possess these things, glamorous or otherwise? I'm often asked why I don't bring my mother's "beautiful things" and my father's "interesting curiosities" to the faraway (in more ways than one) place where I now live. But I think well, what good would that do? They're all still with me in my mind, even more in my heart, perhaps like the way I've always regarded books. Their *possession* has never been a prime interest with me; it's what's *in* the books that matters. And for most of my life I've usually had a great university library at my disposal, often right across the street.

But I think I've been that way about almost all material things my whole life through: I don't want anything that will come to own *me*, anything I have to stay home and take care of. Strange, many people will say—and indeed have said, especially with my interests in literature and the other arts. But perhaps I've come to feel, over the years, that the only real things we can ever truly possess are those which, like memories themselves, are finally intangible—and something we can never lose nor anyone ever take away.

And they never call for an encore.

About the author

Raised in Ripley, Tennessee, and educated at Vanderbilt University and Yale University, Robert Drake has taught English at the University of Texas, Northwestern University, and the University of Michigan. Since 1965, Drake has taught at the University of Tennessee in Knoxville, where he is professor of English. *What Will You Do for an Encore?* is his sixth collection of short stories, and in it Drake again returns to the fictional Southern town of Woodville, a place not unlike his own Ripley. Drake has also published a book of criticism on Flannery O'Connor and a family memoir.